Matt Marshall's
Destiny

Matt Marshall's Destiny

Megan Ahasic

READERSMAGNET, LLC

Matt Marshall's Destiny
Copyright © 2018 by Megan Ahasic

Published in the United States of America
ISBN Paperback: 978-1-947765-69-6
ISBN eBook: 978-1-947765-70-2

All rights reserved. No part of this publication may be reproduced, stored in a retrieval system or transmitted in any way by any means, electronic, mechanical, photocopy, recording or otherwise without the prior permission of the author except as provided by USA copyright law.

The opinions expressed by the author are not necessarily those of ReadersMagnet, LLC.

ReadersMagnet, LLC
10620 Treena Street, Suite 230 | San Diego, California, 92131 USA
1.619.354.2576 | www.readersmagnet.com

Book design copyright © 2018 by ReadersMagnet, LLC. All rights reserved.
Cover design by Ericka Walker
Interior design by Shieldon Watson

More Than a Blizzard Haunts Waterford Street

October 1st, 2012

THERE'S SOMETHING LURKING in the silence of a house. Nothing visible, nothing tangible, yet perceptible, Matt Marshall thought. His eyes wandered the walls and ceiling of the upstairs front room as he sprawled out on the futon. The lamp light was useless in dispelling the gloom which descended upon him. Stale laughter vibrated through the air. Whispers of agony climbed down the walls, rushing at him. How much more, he wondered, will it take to shatter me?

The howl of the wind and the glass rattling in the window frame intensified the things roiling inside. The outside world conspired against him, exacerbating his rapid heartbeat. He closed his eyes and rubbed his temples. Bobby and Jeff should be here soon, he remembered. Then these bygone memories would snake their way back to their proper domain.

Why he chose to remain in here he could not say. Everywhere in the house, he felt watched, judged, tormented. It didn't make sense, since he was alone: he never so much as left a door unlocked. Trapped, he mused, in our own house. A shudder passed through him as he rose from the futon. He trudged downstairs, the light still burning behind him. The wind knocked against the house as he sat on the steps.

Come on guys, what's taking so long? He hoped they weren't goofing off on the way. Jodi and Nicole Baker lived a couple of blocks up, and if the guys ran into them, they'd be in no hurry. Groaning, Matt stood and paced. After a minute, he unlocked the door and pulled it open. Cold air poured in. He stepped out onto the porch, shivering. At that moment, a curtain of snow dropped from the sky. Thin flakes showered down in front of him.

Matt gasped, crumpling his shirt collar in his hand. The sight of wispy flakes always made him happy, except tonight. It was only October 1st, which seemed like a terrible omen. Snap out of it, you're acting like a junior high schooler instead of a fifteen-year-old, he chided, heart pounding. His breath rose in front of him as he scanned the street. The flurries thickened, coming even faster. Alarm wrenched through him. He was tempted to go search for the guys, but visibility was worsening by the second. A heavy fog rolled in as snow coated everything in sight.

I'd better call them, he decided. He pulled his cell phone out of his pocket. Dead, he realized, dashing inside to call Bobby. No one answered. He hung up and dialed Jeff's. Neither Bobby nor Jeff had cell phones, a rarity in this day and age. Jeff's mother answered.

"Hi, is Jeff there?" Matt said.

"Hello, Matt. Jeff and Bobby just left. Tell him to call when he gets there. This snowstorm worries me," she replied.

"I will. Thanks, Mrs. Fischer."

He retrieved his coat from the closet underneath the staircase. Pulling it over his shoulders, he hurried onto the porch. The night was darker now, and the streetlights were hard to see through the fog and the snow. The fog's getting worse, he noted. Unease fluttered in his chest. He sat down on the steps, aware of the cold dusting of snow beneath him. After waiting several minutes, the flutter in his chest grew into a rushing beat that pulsed in his neck. Two silhouettes rounded the corner of his street. He held his breath a moment.

"Jeff? Bobby?" he shouted.

Neither shadow made a sound as they crossed to his side of the street and clambered up the sidewalk. As he watched, a lone car turned the corner and idled up the street. Matt paid little attention. The two figures were now at the end of his yard. He waited for them to come up the walk. To his chagrin, they made their way past. He watched them trundle up the neighbor's drive two houses down. It was Mr. and Mrs. Holland, he realized, stifling a smile. The Hollands were fervent walkers, and neither the weather nor their advanced age stopped them.

Shaking all over, he entered the house, intending to make hot cocoa. He paused when he saw the message light blinking on the answering machine. He hit play, relieved to hear Bobby's voice.

"Bro, answer the phone. We tried to walk to your house, but we couldn't see anything out there, so we came back to my place. See you tomorrow."

Tears stung Matt's eyes. Uttering an agitated sigh, he put his coat away and locked the front door. For the first time all day, his mind drifted to his parents. He hoped they were having fun on their way to Florida. They left yesterday for a two week vacation, and every time they did, a nagging, ill-formed notion surfaced from the crevices of his mind that one day they might not return. Shaking his head, he made a cup of hot cocoa, changed his wet pants, and settled on the couch in the family room. He turned the TV on, searching through the digital guide. Nothing was on. Of course not, he thought, moaning.

He flipped to a random channel just to have some noise in the background. It turned out to be a cable news station. He was spacing out when an up and coming politician came on. Matt didn't catch his name right away, but as soon as he saw the cheery young fellow's face, he was rapt with attention. The man blathered on about budget issues that were uninteresting to a teenager like him, but his eyes commanded attention. Those two gray orbs burned with contempt. The rest of his demeanor appeared calm, and his voice was pleasant, but his eyes broadcast hatred with extreme clarity.

Even worse, Matt noticed that the reporter interviewing him had no clue of the storm brewing inside him. A chill slithered down his spine. He shook his head in response. He didn't know this guy, whose name now flashed at the bottom of the screen. Why should he be concerned? Yet he turned up the volume to better hear what this fellow—Norm Morriston—was saying.

"Is it—do you go by Norm or Norman, Congressman?" the reporter asked.

Matt scowled. He hated when journalists asked pointless drivel like that.

"Just Norm. I'm a regular guy. I want my constituents to address me as they would anyone else."

"There you have it. Norm Morriston from Indiana's seventh district. Thank you, Congressman. I'm Guy Halstadt, live from Washington."

Seventh district? That's our area. Who voted for this windbag, he wondered. He doesn't fool me. The guy's an arrogant piece of work. The moment he conjured up these words, Norm turned and glared into the camera. For a second, he swore Morriston knew his thoughts. The politician's eyes seemed to focus their hatred toward him. He gulped, unable to deny that Morriston was aware of him. Oh come on, he protested, what would he know of a kid like me? Norm's gray eyes flickered with deepening rage. It might have been a flicker of studio lighting, but Matt didn't think so.

For one thing, the host of the program had set up a commercial break, but the broadcast lingered uninterrupted. The cameraman's attention on Morriston's face was as intent as Matt's, for the camera hadn't panned away, even though he said nothing. The anchor had fallen dead silent. The camera rolled for thirty seconds before the break came. The cutaway was severe. Matt pressed the off button as hard as he could, heart jackhammering in his throat.

Attempts to quell his racing heart failed at first. He sipped cocoa, lost in thought. It was almost ten o'clock when he roused himself and glanced at the clock. He gasped and shot up, then recalled that it was Friday night. Still, I better tackle my homework now if the guys are spending the night tomorrow, he thought. A smile dawned on his face. Most people would assume this studiousness meant he was some sort of brain. Though smart, it wasn't a love for his studies that compelled him. His friends, especially his pal Garrett, often teased him about his being somewhat neurotic about certain things. Homework was one of those things. When he finished, it was after midnight. He yawned. Rather than go to bed, Matt turned on the computer, intending to play an online game. When he brought up the internet browser, however, he clicked on a search engine instead. In the box he typed Norm Morriston's name. Only three relevant sites popped up. Matt clicked on one and began reading a brief bio.

"Norman Morriston was born blah, blah, blah. Went to Harvard, majored in Political Science. I see he didn't bother to go the lawyer route. Lives in Moreno, grew up in Bloomsberg. This stupid site tells me nothing about him," he groaned.

After perusing a few short paragraphs on the other sites, he learned zilch about the guy, except that Morriston claimed to be a "values-oriented, open-minded, and fair individual working hard to make the American dream possible for all." How about keeping it alive, Norm, he thought, it's on life-support right now. He shuddered. Where had that come from? He hated politics, and he rarely watched the news, in spite of his aversion to the types of questions some journalists asked. He yawned again and rubbed his eyes. I've got my eye on you, Morriston. Matt turned off the computer and stretched. Before going to bed, however, he checked the sliding door in the kitchen to make sure it was locked and shut the blinds. Then he went down to the basement landing and checked the back door.

He stood facing the door. Dread stole over him. Sensing movement out in the yard, he grabbed the handle. The door was unlocked. I'm positive I locked it earlier, he thought and flipped on the floodlight. Even through the heavy snowfall, he spotted the neighbor's German shepherd moseying through the yard. He was about to go shoo the dog away when the question of how Buster had gotten over the chain link fence occurred to him. What's going on, he wondered. He locked the door and glanced out again. He didn't see anyone, but his field of vision was only about ten feet. His eyes shifted to the fence gate.

The gate was closed. Matt gulped. I'm not going out there, he decided. Let Mr. Welker come get him when he starts barking. Questions commanded his attention. Who let the Buster in and why? For that matter, how did that person get him inside the fence? The gate hadn't been used. If it had, the snow on one side would be disturbed. Both sides were packed with an inch of unblemished snow. And Buster surely hadn't been out there very long: his fur was barely dusted with snow. It occurred to him that someone had let the dog into the yard to lure him out—or to distract him while someone snuck up behind him.

Matt whirled around. No one was there. His face burned with humiliation. Rolling his eyes, he pulled on the door to make sure the lock was engaged and turned off the floodlight. What if someone's out front, he thought. He didn't know why paranoia had invaded him tonight, but he bolted to the front door, eyes zeroing in on the knob.

It was locked. He paused, keenly aware that not enough of the porch was visible from the windows to see if someone lay in wait. Holding his breath, he unlocked the door, eased it open a crack, and peered out. Darkness greeted him. He opened it a little wider, sucking in a deep breath. His fingers groped the switch plate, fumbling for the porch light. A thud arose outside. He strained to hear, but everything went quiet. Light washed over the porch, and he swept his eyes left and right. All was in order. His hands trembled as he opened the screen door. Leaning out, he craned his neck to see. Again, no one was there. Well, why should there be, he scolded. Then he noticed fading footsteps on the porch. He gasped, whipping his head from side to side until he remembered that these were his own tracks from earlier.

I'll chalk that up to lack of sleep, he decided, closing the door and relocking it. He went upstairs, stopping to turn off the light in the front room. In his room, he grabbed his Louisville Slugger and slid it under the sheet beside him. It took a few hours, but at last his eyes started to close. Just as he drifted off, a high-pitched yelp roused him.

It sounded like a dog whimpering. Buster, he thought. He jerked out of bed and stepped to the window. Tearing back the curtains, he gazed out. He couldn't see much of anything down there through the darkness.

Matt turned and scrambled down the hall and the stairwell, across the first floor, and down to the back landing. The floodlight blazed on at his touch. It had stopped snowing, but there was no sign of the shepherd. Glancing at the gate, he saw that it was still undisturbed. He surveyed the yard again. There were no signs that anyone had been here, save for the trench-like paths that ran all over the yard, forged by Buster trotting through the snow. How did Buster get out, Matt wondered as he trudged up to the kitchen. He opened the blinds and peeked out the sliding door. Seeing nothing of note, he reclosed the blinds. When he got to the front door, he stopped and took a gander out at the street. There appeared to be a foot of snow out there. The road had not been plowed yet, though snowplows could be heard working their way down the highway. He sighed and retreated upstairs. This is gonna be a long night, he realized, clutching his bat. In spite of this assumption, he conked out in less than an hour.

At 5:30 a.m., a car struggling for traction in the snow woke him. His heart slammed against his ribs. The car gained traction at last and slipped away. Matt wrestled with his nerves, wishing desperately for a bazooka. He lay still, holding his breath, and listened, heart thrumming a frantic tune. The quiet was overwhelming. Groaning, he rolled out of bed and walked to the end of the hall, where he stood before the double-paned window and peered out. He didn't see any cars, but there were tire tracks on the plowed road and at the edge of his driveway. Perhaps someone had tried to pull into his drive to turn around and had gotten stuck in the snow. Whoever it was had managed to back out, apparently. His blood froze. Something about that scenario felt wrong. He stumbled to his room and grabbed the bat, fastening his fingers around it in a death grip.

Half an hour later, he sat up as sun rose. Bat in hand, he opened the attic door, which was accessed from his room, and ascended the stairs. He held the bat high, ready to defend himself. Despite the clutter in the attic, he searched it in just a few minutes. All clear. He meandered down to his room. I should search all the rooms up here as well. Matt looked through each room, bathroom, and closet, discovering nothing out of the ordinary. So he crept downstairs, gripping the bat tight.

There were no sounds other than his movement and the creaks of the house settling. Bat poised, he made a thorough circuit of the first floor and found everything undisturbed. There was one last place to check: the basement. Gulping, he continued down the back steps, pausing on the landing. His eyes landed on the door. Still locked. Matt looked out at the yard.

The fence gate remained untouched. Buster's paths littered the yard, but the dog had not returned. I better get on with it, he thought. There was no reason for anyone to hide in the basement. He didn't even like going down there. It reminded him of a dungeon divided into four rooms, each featuring a battered concrete floor and crumbling brick walls. The worst was the old root cellar full of ancient dirt. Matt switched on all the lights as he moved through each grimy room. It took little time to confirm the basement was unoccupied.

He switched off the lights and went to poke around the driveway. As he gazed down at the tracks, he had difficulty accepting what seemed a reasonable conclusion: that someone had used the drive to turn around. It struck him as a deliberate warning. Norm Morriston's face flashed through his mind. I can't actually believe that somehow Morriston sent someone after me during a blizzard, can I, he wondered. For this to be true, Norm would have to have known who he was beforehand. And even so, why come after me, Matt mused. The notion was ridiculous. He let out a long breath of relief and chuckled at this absurd paranoia. The respite was brief, however, because in spite of this welcome bit of logic, he could not shake the suspicion that Norm Morriston meant trouble for him.

The Master of Melee

At ten o'clock, Bobby pounded on the front door.

"You know, just once you could leave the door unlocked for us. We'll freeze to death yet," Bobby griped when Matt opened the door.

"Sorry," he said.

Noticing the bags under Matt's eyes, Jeff said, "Trouble sleeping again?"

He nodded.

Bobby narrowed his eyes. "You okay?"

"Yeah, sure." He shrugged.

"Well then, how about feeding us breakfast?" Bobby returned.

Matt gawked at him. "Didn't you eat before you left your house?"

"You know my mom. I swear the highlight of her day is visiting the grocery store. She never keeps much food on hand."

"Oh, she does," Jeff added, "but Bobby consumes it all."

Matt smirked.

Bobby pushed past him. "No fooling, bud, it's cold out here."

"I know. I was out there at 6:30 this morning."

"That's inhuman. Why were you up so early?" Jeff asked.

"I had to check something."

"What?" Jeff inquired.

"I'll explain later."

"Fine. Can we please have something to eat now? I'm starving."

"Sure. There's cereal or Pop Tarts," Matt said.

"Breakfast of champions," Bobby added.

After he ate, they wandered up to Matt's room to play video games. Before they started, he looked at them and said, "Did any of you catch the news last night?"

"No. Why?" Jeff asked.

Bobby rolled his eyes and interrupted, "Dude, the news? Lame."

"I know, but there was nothing else on."

"He's right about that, Bob," Jeff agreed.

"Don't call me Bob," Bobby retorted.

"What's so important about the news?"

"There was this politician on, and he was out there," Matt confided.

"Ooh, spooky. Don't get paranoid on us, man. It's bad enough you think your house is haunted, plus you get all neurotic whenever your parents leave," Bobby said.

Ignoring this, he went on, "After I got your call, I was watching the news, and this congressman, Norm Morriston, came on. The guy was just off. As soon as I realized this, he turned and scowled into the camera as if he knew my thoughts. Then the camera froze on his face without a sound, because the anchor had set up a commercial break. After thirty seconds of soundless air time, it cut to commercial. I shut the TV off. That would have been the end of it, but some strange things happened later."

"Like?" Jeff said.

"For starters, when I checked the back door, it was unlocked, even though I locked it earlier. Then I saw Mr. Welker's German shepherd in the backyard. I don't know how he got inside the fence. The gate was closed, and the snow around it was untouched. And—"

"So Norm Morriston must be conspiring against you, is that it? You're acting like a head case," Bobby interrupted.

"You don't have to be a jerk," Matt complained. He looked at Jeff.

"I'm afraid I agree with him," Jeff said. "There's no way this guy even knows who you are. Even if he did, why would he conspire against you? You're no threat to him. You can't even vote."

"I don't know," he admitted. "But I think we should keep an eye on him."

"Sure," Bobby said. "Let me just get my spy gear," he added.

Matt chucked a pillow at him. Bobby feigned offense, which resulted in a scuffle that Matt lost.

"See? You should work out more, bud. You're a toothpick compared to me."

"Well, I'm quicker and smarter. All you've got is strength, Jock-boy."

Jeff laughed. "Smarter than Bob? Don't think so. He's got straight As, just doesn't like to show it. Do ya, Bob?"

"Don't call me Bob. It makes me sound like I'm an old man walking around in bib overalls. I'm smart, but no nerd. I'd rather stomp guys on the field."

"Our football hero," Jeff exclaimed.

"It's better than your favorite sport, if you can call Shop class a sport, that is."

"I want to be an architect, so I'm working toward my future in a sort of relevant way. Besides, I like building things."

"You also enjoy destroying the things you build," Bobby pointed out.

Matt mimicked Jeff's sister. "Ugh, it must be a guy thing. Blowing up everything and breaking things. You're just lucky it's your stuff. Because if it wasn't, well, I'm not visiting you in prison."

"You sound just like her," Bobby said, laughing.

"I'm disturbed on multiple levels," Jeff added.

Matt smirked. "So am I. This means I've paid way too much attention to her."

"You got that right," Jeff agreed.

The conversation died as soon as they started Resident Evil 6, a zombie horror game. A couple hours later, they took a break to go get snacks from a nearby store, slogging through a foot of snow until they arrived at BG's Breads.

"What are you guys getting?" Matt asked.

"Chips and donuts," Bobby said.

"Yuck. I've got my eye on the beef jerky. What about you, Matt?"

"Not much. Case of soda and some cheese balls."

"Ha, you always get cheese balls to go along with game night, ever since we used to play Donkey Kong Country 3 on my brother's old Super Nintendo. That level with the things that shoot fireballs. They did look like cheese balls," Jeff remarked.

"Yep."

"Our boy's not just funky, he's also cheesy," Bobby joked.

Jeff snorted and said, "Ours? No, I think he's mine. I raised you right, didn't I?"

"Come on, guys. Stop," Matt murmured as they approached the counter.

Thelma, the clerk, smiled as she rang up their purchases. "I'm amazed you boys came out in this. Strange to have such a huge snow so early in the fall, don't you think?"

"It does seem odd," Matt agreed.

When they returned to the house, Matt's neighbor accosted them.

"Morning, Mr. Welker." Matt greeted him with a smile, but his blood pressure skyrocketed.

"Hello, boys. Matt, have you seen Buster anywhere?"

"No, why?" he said.

"It's so strange. He was in the house when I went to bed. This morning, I called for him, but he was nowhere to be found. I don't know how he got out, but he's gotta be somewhere. Weird thing is all the doors were still locked when I got up."

"That is strange," Matt agreed.

"If you see him, let me know. I'm very worried."

"Can do, Mr. Welker. We'll keep an eye out."

"Thanks. I'm gonna drive around the neighborhood, see if I can find him." Mr. Welker headed for his car.

Matt trained his eyes on Bobby and Jeff. "So guys, what do you think of Soul Reaper 3?"

"Why are you asking about that?" Bobby wondered.

"I want to know if it's worth playing."

"Great graphics. Lame weapons. Story is boring too," Jeff answered.

"Really? What did you think, Bob?"

"Don't call me Bob. It was sub-par. Soul Reaper 2 was clearly the better game."

"Oh right. It was pretty awesome. Best of the series," Matt rambled. When Mr. Welker drove off, he raced to the back gate.

"Dude, what is up?" Bobby demanded.

"I want to check out the perimeter, so I can see how Buster got in, preferably before Mr. Welker returns."

"Why didn't you tell him you saw his dog last night?" Bobby asked.

"Now how's he supposed to explain that?" Jeff said.

"Guess it would sound far-fetched," muttered Bobby. "Can we go inside while you're doing that?"

"Sure, Bobby. I don't need any help."

"You sure you don't need protection from the phantoms out there," Bobby called as he walked toward the house.

Jeff poked him. "Lay off."

"Yes, Mother."

"Watch it. I may not be as strong as you, but I have a mean right hook," Jeff threatened.

Bobby threw his hands up. "Ooh, I'm scared."

Matt trudged through the snow around the perimeter. He found no evidence of Buster or anyone else along the inside or outside of the fence line. At the back of the fence, he peered over the large woodpile. Nothing unusual jumped out at him. As he headed back to the house, questions crowded in. He shut them out. In the kitchen, Bobby was munching on a snack.

"Find what you were looking for?" Jeff asked.

"No, nothing."

"How could there be no evidence of how Buster got in and out," Bobby said.

"Finally interested, are you, Bob?" Jeff asked.

Ignoring Jeff, he continued, "Unless—"

"Unless what?" Matt said.

"Unless the dog was air-lifted away. Maybe he was dropped into the yard and lifted away."

"That doesn't make sense. There's no indentation where a platform or a box would have been dropped," Matt pointed out.

"What if he was hooked to a harness and controlled from a helicopter above?" Bobby suggested.

"No way. I would've heard the helicopter hovering overheard."

"He could have been dropped from a plane. Maybe he had a harness with a parachute attached."

"Now who's got the crazy ideas? Don't you think Matt would have seen the harness and the parachute hanging from it?" Jeff added.

"You come up with a theory then," Bobby snapped.

"There is no theory for this. This is madness."

"Tell me about it," Matt groaned. He ran his hands through his hair.

"I hesitate to bring this up, but if anyone could help you, it'd be the Master of Melee. You should give Garrett a call," Bobby proposed.

Matt grinned. "Good idea. He was busy last night, but he's probably free today. With his creativity, we're sure to come up with answers."

"By creative, you mean weird, right?" Jeff added.

"Right," he replied.

Matt picked up the phone and dialed Gar's number. Garrett had been Matt's best friend since kindergarten. He lived across town, but maybe he could get a ride.

"Matt? Is that my dear friend Matthew?" answered Garrett.

"Are you free to come spend the night? I've got a problem that requires your skills."

"I am free. Free to come and aid you in your quest in life, Matthew. Having trouble with Resident Evil 6 again?"

"Negative. Real life situation requires your immediate attention."

"Yeah, because I'm so good at that. That's my strongest point in life, you know. Look, if this is about your love life, or lack thereof, I'm not sure I can help. As I've told you before, I believe you to be a hopeless case."

"Can you come or not?" Matt demanded.

"Be there ASAP. Garrett out."

"Affirmative." Matt hung up.

"From the sound of it, he's still as weird as ever," Jeff said.

Matt nodded.

"You have some strange friends, bro," Bobby noted.

"Yeah, Bob, look as us."

"I fully agree with your statement. And don't call me Bob, Jefferson."

Jeff shoved him. "Call me Jefferson ever again and you die."

He smirked. "At least I don't call you Jeffrey like Garrett does."

Jeff rolled his eyes. "Ugh, I hate it when he does that. But at least that is my actual name, Bob. Strange. I still find him more annoying than you."

"I agree," Bobby said, grinning.

"Say what you guys want, but I'm glad he's coming," Matt told them.

"Me too," Bobby admitted.

Garrett arrived forty minutes later, gasping, brown hair dripping with sweat, pale skin blushed from the cold. Matt gawked at him from the doorway.

"Gar, did you walk here?" he asked.

"Yes and no. I tried to run part of the way, which I deeply regret, and I walked the rest. Mom is taking care of little brother."

"Is he all right?"

"Milo has pneumonia, but he'll be fine. Mom's worried, though. She refused to drive me, because she didn't want to bring him, and Dad's working overtime, so she couldn't leave him at home. She had no problem with me walking all the way here in this bloody cold, however, though she did treat me like I was five years old and make me wear Dad's heavy coat. I told her my winter coat was adequate, but she insisted. And here I am. You have a look of desperation about you, Mattie."

"Yeah, I am desperate. I'm glad you're here."

"Might be nice if you invited me in, so I could warm myself at your hearth," Garrett added, raising his eyebrows.

"Come on in."

As he entered he said, "Right. Let's see what we got going on around here. Hi, Bobby, Jeff."

"Hey, man," greeted Bobby.

"Hello, Master of Melee," said Jeff.

Garrett cracked a smile. "Do you realize that the acronym for that is M.O.M.? Is that what I am now?" he said.

"I never put that together," Jeff confessed.

"I'm entirely unsurprised," Garrett added.

"Maybe we should get down to business," Matt said.

"Oh, so that's how it is. You, good sir, are full of attitudes which are horrid and rude. That's how it's gonna be, eh? Make me walk all the way here in the bloody cold, trudging through mountains of snow, and you won't even let me warm up. You could at least offer me some hot cocoa, you know."

"Fine. You stay here, and I'll make some."

"Do you require my help with that, or would you prefer that to be a solo venture?"

"Knock it off, Gar. I'll get your bloody hot cocoa," Matt retorted.

"Don't say bloody. That's my catch phrase. Plus, it's only funny when I say it."

"Fine."

Matt sauntered away, and Garrett turned to Bobby and Jeff. "Rudeness, I tell you," he said.

"How was that helpful?" Bobby challenged.

"I'm not certain it was, sir. I quite enjoyed it, though. I quite enjoyed it a lot."

"That's obvious," Jeff said.

"What do you mean?" Garrett asked.

"I mean that you're certainly not subtle."

"Are you accusing me of being shallow?" He turned to Bobby, pointing at Jeff. "He's accusing me of being shallow."

Matt smiled as he finished the hot chocolate. He carried the cup into the family room. Garrett snatched it from his hands.

"Give me. Mine. Hot cocoa. Woohoo," Garrett yelled.

"I think giving him sugar may be a bad idea," Bobby said.

"It seems to be agitating him," Jeff observed.

Garrett downed a swig of hot chocolate and set the cup on the table. He sashayed around the room, head down, hand on his chin. He paused momentarily in the center of the room then paced. Matt smirked. Gar's pretending to be Sherlock Holmes again, he thought. He grabbed Garrett's arm. Garrett sat on the hearth, staring at him.

"So what is this problem that has so vexed you that you would turn to me for assistance?"

"Well, last night, I was watching the news," he began.

Garrett put a hand on Matt's forehead. "You watched the news? Quick, does anyone know CPR? Call an ambulance."

"Focus, Gar. There was nothing else on."

"So instead of putting in a DVD or a Blue-ray, you chose the news? It's worse than I thought. Zombie aliens have taken over Matt Marshall's brain. Don't worry. I shall fix you in no time." He tapped on Matt's head and pretended to look in his ear. "Regrettably, there are no signs of life in here."

"Can I continue now?"

"Yes, you may. Do go on."

Matt explained about Norm Morriston and Buster and the lack of footprints around the fence. Garrett was silent. Several minutes went by.

Exasperated, Matt said, "Any ideas?"

"This is a rather sticky situation, isn't it? I'm thinking," Garrett replied.

"Can you think while we take turns on the PlayStation upstairs?"

"May I take my cocoa with me?"

"Yeah."

"Then yes. With the power of this hot chocolate, I shall come up with answers. Or fail. But either way: cocoa."

On the way upstairs, Bobby said, "If you make us play Soul Reaper 3, I'm gonna pound you, Matt."

"He doesn't want to play Soul Reaper, dummy," Jeff replied.

"What's wrong with Soul Reaper 3? Sure, the weapons suck, and it's tame. Is that any reason to get so down on it? Poor game. You're not wanted here. You must vacate the premises immediately," Garrett added.

"Don't lecture us. Just because we demand quality, and you'll play anything that comes along, is no reason to be so high and mighty," Jeff said.

"I believe the word you're looking for is sanctimonious," Matt told him.

"Gee, thanks for defending me, Mattie," Garrett shot back. He raised his eyebrows in an appalled manner.

"You guys pick out what you want to play," Matt said, ignoring Garrett.

"Fine by me," mumbled Bobby.

He and Jeff shuffled through the games. They decided to play each other in a combat game. Garrett sat on the bed next to Matt. When the others were absorbed in the game, he poked Matt and pointed toward the door. Matt followed.

"We should hook up the PlayStation downstairs. It would be a little cozier."

"Later, Gar. What do you want to talk about? Did you figure something out?"

"Matt, I'm not Einstein. But you seemed reluctant earlier to tell me your take on things. I gather Bobby and Jeff made you uncomfortable. So what is it? You mentioned that you think these events are connected to this Morriston chap. You think he's got people fulfilling a hidden agenda against you?"

Matt nodded.

"There's more to it than that, I presume."

Again, he nodded. "That snowstorm coming on so quick like that before Bobby and Jeff came, as if," he trailed off.

"As if it were an attempt to keep you isolated," Garrett finished.

A blush crept over his face, but he nodded.

"If we factor that in, that would mean someone not only knows who you are and is working against you, but that they—or whoever—have the means to effect the weather. This would also mean that they know you quite well, including not just your plans, but your habits."

Matt's eyes widened. "What do you mean?"

"Come on, you intuited that when you thought someone was using the dog to lure you out. The perpetrator had to know that you check the doors every night to make sure they're locked. Therefore, you've been observed for some time, or so this implies."

"It sounds super paranoid," grumbled Matt. "I'm sorry for you wasting your time, Gar. This is just stupid."

Garrett put a hand on his shoulder. "Now wait a minute. All the years I've known you, you've never reacted irrationally without good reason. I believe you may be right that someone is targeting you. I want to know why."

"Does that mean you take me seriously?" he said.

Garrett nodded, removing his hand from Matt's shoulder. "I always do, Matthew. Besides, you can't rule out the impossible unless you prove it impossible. You know I like to consider each intriguing angle. Also, I like mysteries." He clapped his hands.

"I'm lucky you're here."

"Don't get mushy yet. There's an obvious fact here. As yet, it is unspoken, but you may not like it."

"What's that?"

"If we accept the current premises, there is no conceivable motive for these attacks on you. Yet."

Matt groaned.

"Whoever is doing this sees you as a threat."

"I figured that, but I haven't done anything to anyone."

"Let me finish. Since you never say boo to anyone, I think it's safe to assume that it is not what you have done, but what you might do that has earned you such ire."

"What? Are you suggesting a time travel thing?" He wrinkled his brow.

"No. I'm saying that whoever is torturing you this way is afraid of your potential."

"What potential? And how could that be dangerous to anyone?"

"That is what you must figure out."

"That seems unlikely."

"This whole thing seems unlikely," Garrett agreed, "but we must at least consider it as a motive."

"I suppose we do."

"Shall we go back and watch Bobby and Jeff duel each other?"

"Yeah. Let's go."

Garrett led the way, lost in thought. Matt sighed. At least someone took him at his word. Bobby and Jeff were unaware that they had ever left.

"Matt, be a good host, and go get us some sodas," Jeff pleaded.

"I'm all for that," Bobby added.

"I am also in favor with this notion," Garrett said.

"Thanks, Gar," Matt muttered, glaring at him.

"You're welcome," Garrett responded, a silly grin on his face.

Matt rolled his eyes and headed downstairs. When he entered the kitchen, he saw that it was eight o'clock. Wow, I can't believe none of us is hungry yet. Bobby and Jeff had eaten their snacks, but he still expected them to come running down, begging him for sustenance. A flash of light outside the sliding door caught his eye. Matt jumped, clapping his hand over his mouth to keep from shrieking. He stumbled, regained his balance, and fumbled to open the blinds, his heart racing. Then he spotted the source of the light: headlights on the nearby highway. A shaky breath rushed out of his parted lips. Nothing's out there, he thought. As if to prove this, he opened the door, stepped onto the stoop, and glanced around. No one was out there, not even Buster.

He sighed, staring at the sky. Stars glittered above him, making him smile. Amazing, he mused, absolutely amazing. He closed his eyes for a few minutes taking in the night air. Another flash of light snared his attention. It was red instead of white. His eyes flew open. He searched for the source of it and gaped as his gaze lifted to the sky. A large, red target sign glowed above him. His throat closed up, and cold sweat slathered his flesh, sending chills through him. A certainty that defied explanation stole over him.

He knew that the target was meant for his eyes only. The all-consuming menace of the sight left no room for doubt in his mind. As the target sign faded, Matt opened the sliding door and shoved himself inside. He moved so fast that his feet slid, and he sprawled on the kitchen floor, stomach whacking the linoleum. Unaware of the blow, he flopped onto his back, scuttling away from the open door. Shallow pants broke through his lips.

"Matt?"

He stifled a scream as Garrett morphed out of the darkened doorway and into the kitchen.

"What is it?" Garrett asked, noting his pale face and sweat-mussed hair.

Matt breathed hard, cringing against the side of the fridge. His eyes returned to the open door. He wrapped his arms around himself. Garrett shut the door and crouched in front of him.

"What're you doing?"

"Garrett, what're you doing down here?"

"Jeff and Bobby kept throwing things at me until I agreed to come light a fire under you. Now what happened?"

A hoarse laugh escaped him. "I got jumpy, because I saw something outside, which turned out to be headlights, so I went out to prove that nothing was there."

Garrett grinned. "Did you find Buster or something?"

Matt shook his head. "No. I was looking at the stars. I closed my eyes for five minutes or so, and there was a flash of red." He paused for breath.

"Ooh, intrigue."

"When I opened my eyes, there was a huge target sign in the sky."

"You think it's related to the previous events?"

"You believe me?" Matt asked.

"I told you before. I don't think you're quackers or anything."

"Thanks."

"Yeah. You should probably get up. I imagine the floor is cold." He held out his hand.

"What now?"

"I don't know." Garrett walked through the threshold, sat at the desk, and turned on the computer.

"What're you doing?"

"I need to think. The best way to do that is gaming."

"Don't you want to use the PlayStation? It's our turn, anyway."

"I want to play a computer game. Nostalgia."

"Let me pull up a chair, and I'll watch."

"You'll be witnessing a master at work," Garrett uttered, cracking his knuckles.

"The Master of Melee strikes again."

"What a stupid nickname."

"Fine. I won't call you that," Matt promised.

"But I love that nickname," he whined.

"You just said it was stupid."

"That's why I like it."

Matt rolled his eyes. Bobby and Jeff wandered down a few minutes later.

"Here they are, playing computer," Jeff remarked.

"Where's our soda," Bobby demanded.

"In the fridge, naturally," Garrett noted.

"Why'd you say you'd get us a soda if you weren't coming back?" grumbled Bobby.

"Because he was coerced into that mission," Garrett pointed out.

"You helped them, Gar," Matt retorted.

"True," he confessed. "But I became your ally the moment they started throwing things at me, good sir."

"Whatever. We'll get it ourselves," Jeff muttered.

"I'm hungry," Bobby murmured.

"Yeah, when are you going to get us dinner?" Garrett asked.

Matt groaned. "I'll order a pizza."

"Ooh, pizza. Yes." Garrett pumped his arms up and down.

Around midnight, they called it a night. Bobby took Matt's room, Jeff opted for the guest room due to Bobby's snoring, which left Garrett to curl up on the futon in the front room. Matt settled for the couch downstairs. His eyes flicked over the ceiling. He figured the quiet that descended over the house was too good to last, and he was right.

A wave of nausea hit him as the wind barraged the house. Groans issued from the old boards as the house shook. Shivers wracked his body. I wish Gar was down here, he thought. The last few nights, strange things had occurred, some related to the house, some not. Matt cut his mind off before he could dredge it up.

When the wind died at last, his eyes grew heavy and closed. A thud overhead brought his eyelids up once more. It sounded as if a cat had jumped off the bed onto the floor of his parents' room above. He drew in a shaky breath and turned onto his side, face pressed against the back of the couch.

He was almost out when a wailing noise broke the silence. The cries surrounded him, growing louder by the second. He cringed, head spinning. That's a baby howling, he realized, but none of the neighbors have kids. This had happened before. It was part of a series of strange events that had started in the last week. Goosebumps broke out over his arms. Matt covered his ears with trembling hands. The whine pierced him. Pain lashed through his sides. He held his breath. The undead scream multiplied into a chorus of shrieking voices. He pulled his hands away from his ears and yanked the blanket over his head. Please God, let it go away, he prayed. Please protect me.

The horrific sounds stopped. He dropped his twitching hands and let out a pent up breath. Just as he threw the blanket off his head, a series of noises boomed. He knew the commotion well: it was someone running up and down the basement steps. He'd heard his dad run up and down them a million times fetching his power tools during a project. Why didn't I bring the bat down, he wondered. He didn't want to investigate, but it had to be done, for his sanity, at least. As he rose, the sound died away.

Matt halted in front of the basement door. No going back now, he thought, yanking the door open. When he flipped the light on, there was no one on the stairs or the landing. He inched down the four steps to the back door. Still locked. Turning, he switched on the basement light. Nothing. I'll have to check the entire basement, he realized. There was no way. Not by himself, and not without a weapon. He raced back to the kitchen and tore through the first floor to the staircase. With eerie stealth, he slipped upstairs and shook Garrett.

"What's with all the bloody shaking?" Garrett mumbled.

"I need your help."

Garrett sat up, stretched, and yawned. He glanced at the glowing numbers on his digital watch. "Matt, it's one-thirty in the morning. I just fell asleep."

"Sorry, but I need your help."

Grunting, Garrett followed him downstairs. "This bloody house," he remarked. "It's always something."

Matt relaxed a little as he explained what happened. Gar knew of his prior experiences and would not confuse this event with the Morriston related occurrences that had plagued him the last two days.

"We're checking the basement, then?" Garrett rubbed his eyes.

"Yep."

"Lucky I'm always here for you, Mattie."

"I know, I know. I totally owe you."

"Mm, yes, totally," he said.

Matt led the way to the back landing. On the last step, Garrett pulled him back. Matt shuddered. That crying baby noise filled his ears, sounding muffled and faraway. It stopped all of a sudden, as if cut off. He turned toward Garrett, who held a finger to his lips, then pointed to the kitchen. They crept back up the stairs.

"What is it?" he whispered as they came into the kitchen.

Garrett spoke not a word. Instead, he pointed at the knife holder. Matt grabbed a long carving knife and returned to the basement door. He paused.

"Did you hear something down there? Is that why you stopped me?"

Garrett nodded.

"What'd you hear?"

"For cripe's sake, let's get going before I lose my nerve," he muttered.

Matt sneaked down to the landing. His eyes paused on the locked door knob for a moment. Garrett followed his gaze then prodded his shoulder. At the bottom of the stairs, they glanced around the room. It was a small area, and they quickly confirmed its vacancy. No intruder could be concealed unnoticed behind the stairs, either, because the gaps between each step allowed them to see behind it.

"Next room," Matt murmured, flipping on the light in the furnace room.

Garrett nodded, his eyes trained ahead of Matt. They cleared the furnace room with a sweeping glance. An intruder would be revealed straightaway in the 10x10 space. Garrett leaned right, peering between the furnace and the wall to the root cellar. Beads of sweat broke out on his brow. Empty shadows greeted him. He sighed with relief.

Matt held his breath as they entered the third room. He zipped forward and grasped for the light. When he found the pull string, he yanked it so hard, it almost came right off. He whipped his head to and fro. He didn't see anyone, but this was the largest room, and half of it remained dark. Another light was located at the other end near the fuse box. Once that light was on, they would be vulnerable. It was in the sightline of the entrance to the root cellar, which would be a perfect place for someone to hide.

Matt took a deep breath. Garrett leaned forward and whispered in his ear, "Either get moving, or stand aside so I can."

Garrett shoved him forward. At that moment, Matt recalled the knife in his hand. Gar was defenseless. That got him moving. He slashed at the darkness with the knife until he reached the light. When he pulled the string and turned toward the root cellar, the doorway was black and empty. He let out a pent up breath. Garrett grabbed the knife from his shaking hands.

"You stay here," Garrett said.

"You can't go in there alone."

"You're too jumpy. I tried to walk beside you, and you nearly diced me, waving that knife around," he whispered.

Matt watched with wide eyes as Garrett approached the doorway. Without hesitating, he slipped inside. Matt waited, unable to see him. Moments passed. He strained his ears, but heard nothing. Be careful, Gar, he thought. Light flooded the room. Matt cried out.

"Calm yourself, Matthew. There's no one in here," Garrett called.

He was still putting it together that the root cellar had a light when Garrett emerged.

"Come see for yourself."

Matt went inside, ducking his head as he entered. He stood in the dirt and looked around. Nothing was out of place.

"I'm sorry, Gar. This was dumb."

"No, it wasn't. Come on, let's get out of here."

Garrett stopped on the landing and flipped on the outside floodlight.

"What?" Matt asked.

"I just wanted to make sure there was no one out in the yard. Or any dogs."

Matt squinted at him. Garrett, pale and sweaty, held the knife up in front of him. His knuckles were white from gripping the handle so tight. Something freaked him out, Matt realized. Garrett switched off the light and proceeded to the kitchen.

"Tell me what you heard when we started down," Matt asked.

"I thought I heard movement."

"Really? I didn't hear anything. Could it have been us?"

"No. Because I also heard rustling noises, like someone shuffling papers around or going through things."

The color drained from his face. "Did you hear anything else?"

"Well, I thought I heard—never mind."

"Tell me," he insisted.

"It sounded like a child weeping far off in the distance."

Matt cringed. "I heard that, too."

Garrett shook his head. "Enough of this. Matt?"

"Yes?"

"I'm freezing all of a sudden. Would you turn the heat up?"

"The thermostat's on 70, but you're right. It is colder in here."

"Maybe because we've had the basement door open."

He nodded. "Hey, if you want to sleep in the family room, I can make a fire."

Garrett rolled his eyes. "I suppose I can live with your snoring," he said.

Grinning, Matt replied, "I just need to get some wood from out back."

He fetched the plastic tub that he used for hauling in wood. Garrett eyed him curiously. It was too much for him to bear. "What?" he said.

"Let me get my coat," Garrett replied. He let out an exaggerated sigh.

"You're coming with me?"

With his back to Matt, he inquired, "Why do you question me, good sir?"

Matt started. "Sorry, Gar."

"I'll fetch my coat. I shan't be but a moment."

"Alright."

Garrett returned with two coats in his hand. He held Matt's out to him.

"Thanks."

"Don't mention it. Seriously. If my mom finds out she's rubbing off on me, I'll never live it down."

They went outside. The floodlight wasn't great beyond its twenty foot range, but it still allowed them fair enough vision to make their way through the remaining twenty feet of yard. As they pushed through the snow, they noticed something dark splashed across the ground in front of the woodpile.

"What is that?"

"I don't know. I guess it could be mud. Maybe some of the snow melted, although that spot wasn't there earlier."

Garrett grabbed his arm and squeezed hard.

"Dude, let go. You're hurting me."

Garrett's jaw dropped. Matt glanced at him. He pointed down in front of them near the wood pile. Matt shifted his gaze. His blood ran cold. A long choke chain was nestled in that dark spot in the snow.

"Was that there when you checked the perimeter earlier?" Gar asked.

"No," he croaked. "Buster? Here, boy. Here, Buster. Come on, puppy," he whispered.

There was no response.

"Let's take a closer look," Garrett suggested.

Matt's pulse raced as they walked forward. Gawking at the sight, he bit back bile.

"Oh man. It's blood," he said.

"Looks like it's Buster's."

"How do you know that?"

"The collar, for one thing. Plus that," Garrett said, pointing again.

Matt stared past the woodpile and the fence. "Oh no."

There was Buster's mangled body next to a tree. Matt started dry heaving. Garrett managed to catch him when he fell backward, uttering a mental scream that came out as a gasp.

Dangerous Potential

GARRETT TILTED MATT back onto his feet. With a groan, he steadied his legs. Gar stepped up beside him, wide-eyed. The image of Buster all bloody and torn stuck in his mind. Rattling wheezes escaped his lips. Tears blurred his vision for a moment. Matt turned toward him, mouth agape, eyes bloodshot.

"Was that—was that Buster?" he gasped.

"I guess. It has to be him, doesn't it," Gar reasoned.

"Who would do such a thing?"

"A psycho, obviously, or," Garrett began.

"Or what?" Matt interrupted, grabbing hold of him and shaking him.

"Or someone who wants to intimidate you, as we figured before. Maybe even set you up to look crazy."

"Why?"

"I'm not sure yet."

"What are we gonna do?"

"We need to get rid of the body first."

"But what about Mr. Welker?"

"How would you explain this when neither of us has any answers?"

"I don't know," Matt snapped.

"Go in the house and get us some gloves."

"What for?"

"We'll put Buster in the creek back there," Garrett replied, meaning a creek that ran through an abandoned brickyard located behind the property.

Matt sprinted to the house and fetched a box of latex gloves. When he got back, Garrett was kneeling on the other side of the fence, examining Buster's corpse. His eyebrows rose, and his lips parted in a smile. As Matt approached, Garrett narrowed his eyes, but the smile remained.

"What are you doing?" Matt asked.

"Whoever did this gets major props."

"For killing a dog? That's sick." He glowered at Garrett.

"This is not a real dog," answered Garrett.

"What?"

"It's a stuffed animal ripped open and covered in cherry syrup."

"Taxidermy?"

Garrett shook his head. "No, it has synthetic fur and glass eyes."

"Okay, wait. How do you know that this red stuff is cherry syrup and not blood?"

"I tasted it."

Matt gawked. "Ugh," he groaned.

Garrett grinned wider. "Lighten up. I did not sample it, but I did smell it."

Matt grimaced. He knelt in front of the red puddle, sniffing. Garrett was right. He could smell cherry flavoring. As he peered at the stained snow, he saw that it was indeed syrup and not blood. He let out his pent up breath, shaking. The pit of his stomach churned. As he watched, Garrett continued to inspect the stuffed carcass. Matt got to his feet.

"What do we do now?" he asked.

"We've got to clean this up. I suggest you get me some garbage bags."

"Right."

"Matt?"

"Yes?"

"Could you toss me a pair of those gloves, please?"

"Sure." He threw the box over the fence. His aim was off, and the box whacked Garrett in the head.

"Thanks a bunch, Matt."

"Sorry."

He hurried into the house and retrieved two trash bags. Garrett was standing when he got back. He held out his arm.

"Hand those to me. I do not wish to be assaulted again."

Matt rolled his eyes. "There is no way that hurt you."

"You don't realize the force with which you threw that box at me."

"Whatever. Let's just get this over with."

Garrett wrestled the pseudo-dog into the first garbage bag. It stuck out a bit over the top, so he covered it with the other bag. Then he dragged it around to the fence gate, motioning for Matt to meet him at the gate.

"Grab that end. You wouldn't think this thing would be so bloody heavy, but it is."

Matt grabbed it and gasped.

"Told you it was heavy. I don't know what it's stuffed with, but it feels like a medicine ball's in there or something."

Matt stopped. "Maybe we should cut it open and look, Gar."

Garrett groaned. "Fine, but let's do it tomorrow. I would like to get some sleep, you know."

"Agreed. Let's stash it in the basement."

"No. It's coated in syrup, remember? That would make a huge mess. Here, set it down. I wasn't thinking."

Garrett ran to the front of the house and came back dragging one of the garbage cans.

"This'll do, eh, Mattie?"

"Good idea."

They removed the lid, heaved the bundle up and deposited it, retrieved the dog collar and slipped it inside, then replaced the lid. After sliding the can to the side of the house, they put a couple of bricks on top to keep animals from getting at the syrup covered beast.

"Okay, now we get firewood."

"What about cleaning up the syrup?" Matt asked.

"Nature'll take care of that for us. Either that, or we could make snow cones." He beamed at Matt.

"All right, fine."

It took four trips to get enough wood to fill up the alcove next to the fire place, but at last, it was done. Once the fire was lit, Matt lay on the couch. Across the room, Garrett lay snug in Matt's sleeping bag. He suspected that the silence between them was too good to last as soon as Matt turned toward him.

"What do you think this means?" Matt asked.

"I dunno."

"And Buster. Is he still alive?"

Garrett uttered a prolonged groan. "Too many questions. I'll deal with it later."

Matt grunted. "Fine. Sleep if you must, Master of Melee."

Garrett closed his eyes, trying to stifle his curiosity. After a while, he heard Matt's breathing deepen, a sure sign Matt was asleep. But now those questions sent his mind racing. At last, his eyes flew open. Although the fire was still blazing, he shivered. Gotta be brave, he decided. Matt needed someone courageous by his side. He figured he would have to do. Jeff and Bobby were loyal friends, but they were ill-equipped to deal with these peculiarities. For one thing, they were too practical and lacking in imagination. There were certain things that they just refused to consider, even if the evidence was right in front of them.

This called for a unique and intuitive soul, and he fit the bill. Matt had always accepted this, even when he was teased for being friends with Gar. He'd sought Garrett out in kindergarten. Since then, Garrett had stood by him. Goodness, such sappy ponderings, he mused. I must be vexed. In that moment, a weight dropped upon the air. The hushed house quivered with anticipation. The crackling of the fire seemed muted, bowing to the silence. A sudden shriek pulsed through the night.

Garrett's heart galloped in his chest. He'd heard this earlier on the back steps. It sounded like a toddler screaming its lungs out in the distance. Holding his breath, he struggled to pinpoint the sound. It was over too soon for him to ascertain the origin. His mouth fell open, and forced breaths rushed in and out. The only sound he heard now was a log shifting in the fireplace. However, he felt a presence nearby. The certainty that he was being watched permeated his being. His body went rigid. His frayed nerves shouted in protest when he decided to move. It took every ounce of courage within to force himself to sit up. He glanced around. Nothing here, of course, he realized.

At that moment, clear as a bell, a voice whispered, "Accompany him through the darkness."

He bit back a scream, his breath fleeing as he strained his ears. His fingers wound tightly around the fabric of the sleeping bag. His ears sifted through the hushed atmosphere. Grunting, he threw the sleeping bag aside. I need a drink, he decided. In the kitchen, he paused beside the fridge and turned toward the sliding door. His eyes widened. The blinds were open. He had watched Matt close them after he checked to make sure everything was locked earlier. The blinds were pushed back, exposing half of the door. He stared through the glass, adjusting to the sight. Movement drew his attention. A gasp escaped his lips. He backed against the fridge, frozen to the spot.

Buster glared in, teeth bared. Garrett's eyes grew wider as Buster backed up and lunged at the door. He tried to run and failed, eyes locked on Buster. He could not tear them away.

"No," he croaked.

Buster's paws thudded against the glass, and he bounced off. He got up, halting. His ears pricked up. Abruptly, his demeanor changed. As Garrett watched this transformation, his legs grew shaky. His body turned cold, yet at the same time, it felt like his bones were melting. Meanwhile, Buster's ears flattened against his skull. His tail dropped between his legs. A shudder passed through him, and he whimpered. Buster ran at the door again, jumping up. He pawed at the glass, as if trying to get inside.

The shepherd's eyes were wide and frantic. I don't want to see what happens next, Garrett realized. His paralysis broke, and he bolted from the kitchen. He yanked the sleeping bag over his body and squeezed his eyes shut. Buster whined over and over, but he was no longer sure if it was real or in his head. Shivering, he was unable to sleep for a very long time.

The increasing sunlight teased Matt's eyes open. Although all his dreams had been nightmares, he didn't want to get up. A soft moan roused him. He sat up and turned toward Garrett. His brow furrowed. Garrett lay in a fetal position, murmuring. His arms were wrapped around his chest. Sweat glistened on his forehead. Looks like he had a rough night too, Matt thought. He yawned and got up to find something to drink, hoping Bobby and Jeff hadn't absconded with all the soda. He froze just inside the kitchen threshold. The blinds that he'd closed last night were open. He supposed Garrett had opened them, but why?

Stop being so jumpy, he told himself. He probably woke up earlier and wanted to let some sun in. Satisfied, he stepped forward then stopped again. He jerked his head to the left and gawked at the door. Muddy streaks and paw prints were smeared on the glass. He shot off into the family room and shook Garrett.

"Garrett. Gar, wake up," he said.

An unintelligible sound came out of Garrett's mouth, followed by, "What?"

"There are dog tracks on the sliding door."

"Mm. I know. I saw him."

"What? You saw them?"

"Saw Buster," mumbled Garrett.

"When?"

Garrett opened his eyes, yawning. At last, he got up and went into the kitchen, grabbing a soda from the fridge. Matt trailed behind him.

"Is there another one in there?" Matt asked.

"Yep."

"Grab me one, will ya?"

He nodded and handed Matt a soda. "Sit, Matthew, and I shall tell you all I know. You shall have the knowledge that I now have churning within."

"Get to the point."

"After you fell asleep, I got up to fetch a drink. I noticed the blinds were open and peeked out and there's Buster staring at me and growling."

Matt swallowed hard. A huge lump had formed in his throat.

"He lunged at the door. When he backed off, he looked spooked. He whimpered and pawed at the door like crazy. And that's when I ran like a pansy," he finished.

Matt blanched. "So he's alive. What happened to him?"

"I don't know. I really don't want to know, either."

Matt frowned. "I don't get it. Why would someone do this stuff?"

"To mess with you, psyche you out."

"To what end?"

"Guess we'll have to wait and see."

"Gar, yesterday you said that whoever's doing this might be afraid of my potential."

"I recall saying that."

"How is my potential dangerous to anyone?"

Garrett sighed. "I don't know."

"Surely you have some idea."

"We'll figure it out. Calm yourself."

"How can I be calm? I don't have any answers," he groaned.

"Well, if I can act so suave and cool, you could at least attempt to imitate my example."

"Oh yeah, you're so cool," Matt mocked.

Garrett narrowed his eyes. "What is wrong with you?"

"I'm sorry. I just want to know why me?"

"Maybe it's not just you. Maybe there are several people out there that this is happening to who are hiding what's going on. It is a huge world, y'know."

Matt laughed. "That's the most paranoid statement yet."

Garrett grinned. "True. It does sound saucer-kingdomish. But maybe my good friend Matt is the sole victim in this weird game," he added.

Matt smirked. "What's so special about me?"

"Your potential, apparently. You're a threat, and you didn't even know it," Garrett told him, clapping his hands.

"What's so threatening about that, though?"

"That is a question for every dictator and totalitarian ruler on the planet. Why do they fear what people might do, especially those they manipulate and brainwash?"

His question sent a shiver through Matt. Changing the subject, Garrett said, "Come on, let's have some pizza."

"Ooh, pizza," Matt replied.

"I second that," Garrett agreed with a nod.

After they ate, Matt said, "We should examine that faux dog, Gar."

"Yes. Let's. Shall we include Bobby and Jeff?"

A wide smile spread across Matt's face. "Nah."

"Ooh, a secret quest. I like secret quests."

They slipped out the back door. Sunshine washed over them, brightening their spirits. Matt grabbed the garbage can and dragged it over. He gasped.

"Matt? Something wrong?"

"This can is way too light."

They took the lid off and peered inside. The can was empty. The garbage bags were gone, as was the stuffed dog and the collar, and the inside was spotless.

"We should see if that large stain in the yard is still there," Garrett stated.

Matt followed him to the back of the yard. The cherry syrup was indeed gone, and so were their tracks, as well as all the paths Buster had woven through the snow. The snow was smooth and even, as though it had never been touched. They examined the area where they had found the fake Buster. The snow on the ground and the tree, which had been splattered with syrup, was also clean.

"What's going on?" Matt blurted out.

Without comment, Garrett raced to the stoop by the sliding door then returned to Matt. Shaking, he said, "Even that has been cleaned up, except for the door. How could all of this have been cleaned up so fast and so flawlessly?"

"This is so messed up."

"It's bloody creepy, that's what it is."

"You got that right." Matt frowned when he saw Garrett sweating. "What's up?"

"This implies something not good, Mattie."

"What's that?"

Garrett's eyes widened. "This implies that there are multiple people involved in this thing."

Matt shrugged. "Didn't we already assume that?"

"We considered it, but Matt, I think this illustrates that there are more than one or two or even a few people involved."

"I'm not following you."

"Think, Matt. How many people would it take to clean up that cherry syrup in so short a time and even out the snow in this whole yard? And how many to lug the stuffed dog, which took both of us to lift, and how many to clean up the garbage can while the two were carting off that bundle of joy? Then there is the person or persons responsible for putting the real Buster in the yard and making sure one of us would see him. That person also had to get him out of here before we woke up. I imagine that during this distraction, the rest of the crew was working their butts off to make things spotless again."

The color drained from Matt's face. "I never thought of that."

Garrett opened his mouth to speak, when a voice called to them. They turned to see Mr. Welker waving at them from the other side of the fence. Although he wore a friendly smile, he was trembling a bit.

"Matt, I just wanted to let you know that Buster is okay. He must've come back." His voice was a bit screechy.

"He did?"

A sharp bark came from Mr. Welker's left, and there was the wily shepherd. Mr. Welker patted his head. "It's the oddest thing. He was still missing last night, but when I woke this morning, he was on the floor beside the bed, snoozing away. I can't make heads or tails out of it. I got up and checked all the doors and all the windows, and they were all locked up tight."

"Odd," Matt agreed.

"Maybe he was hiding somewhere in the house the whole time," Garrett suggested.

Mr. Welker wrinkled his brow. "Hello, Garrett. No, he wasn't in the house. I checked everywhere."

"That is strange," said Garrett.

"Yes. I think I'm going to have a security system put in, although I've never had any problems with intruders before. It's not like anything was stolen, and I can't be sure anyone has even entered the house. But I guess it's best to protect the premises. Although, that's supposed to be Buster's job," he added with a laugh.

Buster chuffed, an indignant expression on his face. Mr. Welker said goodbye and tugged Buster along. "Come on, boy. If you want to get a walk in before I've had my breakfast, let's get a move on." They trotted away.

"Matt," whispered Garrett.

"Yeah?"

"Let's go inside. We need to talk."

Once inside, Matt looked at him, waiting for him to speak.

"I hate to say this, but we should be wary of Mr. Lawrence Welker."

"Garrett," he warned.

"He might be in on it, Matt."

Matt rolled his eyes. "Oh come on. That doesn't sound paranoid in the least."

"We have to consider it."

"I guess. But I don't like assuming things about my neighbors, especially him. Mr. Welker's been a good neighbor for years."

"I know. And he did seem genuinely shaken, didn't he?"

Matt nodded.

"All right. Assume his innocence, but remain on guard."

Again, Matt nodded.

"Shall we snag the PlayStation before Bobby and Jeff awaken?" Garrett asked.

"I have no objection to this," he said, smirking.

"Ooh, mine. Mine," Gar exclaimed, holding up one of the controllers.

Matt laughed. "Oh, be right back," he said.

"What're you doing?"

"I forgot I have to do laundry."

"Chores? At a time like this?"

Matt shrugged. "I've put it off long enough. But if I want clean clothes for school tomorrow, I'd better wash some stuff. Besides, my P.E. uniform is starting to smell."

"Ew."

"My sentiments exactly," Matt said. He tossed everything into the washer, then dumped in a capful of detergent and started it.

When he returned, he saw that Garrett had chosen the zombie game Bobby and Jeff had played last night.

"Come, Matthew, we shall show these zombie creeps who is the real master of the zombie world."

"You got it, Gar."

Two hours later, Matt remembered to throw the clothes in the dryer. When he left the bathroom, he saw that a sad expression adorned Garrett's face.

"What's wrong?"

"Bobby and Jeff stole our turn on the PlayStation," he whined.

"We could play a compute game."

Garrett shook his head. "Bloody Matt, if only you had X-Box."

Matt rolled his eyes. "You don't have X-Box either. Anyway, what do you want to do?"

"We could go watch them fail at that zombie game. That might make me feel better."

Matt smirked. "Yeah, why don't we?"

Garrett clapped.

Bobby glanced up when they returned. "I see you two weren't gonna get us up. You were gonna keep the zombies all to yourselves," he accused.

Garrett flashed a smug grin back at him. "But of course."

Jeff groaned. "Bobby, why'd you have to start with him? It's too early to deal with that."

"Dude, it's eleven o'clock in the morning. My dad would have a fit. He gets me up at six every morning for my training."

"And now you know why I don't do sports," Jeff replied.

"Hey man, just because you're undisciplined, doesn't mean I should be too."

"Getting up at six in the morning? That's inhuman," moaned Jeff.

"Yes, because Jeffrey likes his sleep, doesn't he? Our little sleepy head. How adorable."

"Shut up, Garrett," Jeff shouted.

"Easy, you two," Matt said.

"Are you guys gonna watch us or what?" Bobby asked.

They sat on the couch, and Jeff turned his attention back to the game.

"It's about time, Jeff. I've only been dying over here."

"Quit your whining, Bob."

"Don't call me Bob."

"Bibbidy bobbidy boo," said Garrett.

Matt punched his arm. "Stop."

"Ow. Stop punching me. That's not nice."

"Neither is being an annoying jerk," he snapped. He regretted this when he saw the look of hurt on Garrett's face. "Sorry, man."

Garrett looked away. "Fine." He slid off the couch and tromped into the kitchen.

Matt followed him. "Gar, where ya going?"

"I'm getting some cocoa. You owe me some cocoa for being a Mr. Meany."

Matt laughed. "Oh. For a second there, I thought you were mad at me."

"I was, a little."

"What can I do to make it up to you?"

"Cocoa. Also, I'm no longer angry." He favored Matt with a toothy grin.

"Okay. The cocoa is in the cabinet."

"Ooh, cabinet cocoa. Is there anything better? Unless it was a cocoa cabinet. That would be sweet."

Matt nodded in agreement. Once Garrett's hot chocolate was ready, they returned to the family room. Bobby and Jeff hadn't gotten very far. They had already died twice.

"You know, Matt and I had no problem with this area."

"Jeff and I wouldn't either if our whole lives revolved around video games too."

"That is why everyone should imitate me. I am a role model for all generations," Garrett stated.

"That's our Master of Melee," Matt added.

A couple of hours later, after Matt turned back the dryer, he and Gar took a turn slaughtering zombies while Jeff and Bobby ate pizza. By two o'clock, Bobby and Jeff were on their way home. Garrett stayed until seven o'clock.

"Matt, you gonna be all right?" he asked before he left.

"I'll be fine. I'll just keep busy."

"All right. Sleep tight, little Mattie, and don't let the bedbugs bite."

Matt rolled his eyes. "Be safe on the way home, M.O.M."

Cracking a smile, he said, "That's Madame M.O.M. to you, good sir."

"Are you sure you don't want my bat to take with you? It's a long walk, and it'll be dark by the time you get home."

"I'll be fine. See you tomorrow."

"See ya," Matt said, closing the door. He locked it and moved to the window, watching Garrett walk away until he was out of sight. He closed his eyes, uttering a quick prayer for Gar to make it home safely.

Then he meandered into the kitchen and checked the sliding door to see if it was locked, closing the blinds afterward. Sighing, he trudged down the back steps. The basement door was already locked. He hadn't even remembered doing it. Matt tugged the door handle to make sure it was secure. His eyes fell on the deadbolt. He hesitated. He almost never locked it, because he didn't have a key to the deadbolt. As he turned the knob to engage it, a thought occurred to him. When he finished, he ran upstairs. In his parents' room was a door that used to lead to a deck. The deck had become unsafe in recent years, so his father took it down and bolted a metal ladder to the side of the house as a fire escape.

This door also had a deadbolt on it. Matt stared at it. It was locked, as he'd expected. He tested the door. The lock was working. Narrowing his eyes, he unlocked the door and opened it, peering down. Seeing nothing, he closed the door and relocked it. Everything's good here, he thought. Guess I should fold my laundry. Of all the chores, laundry was his least favorite. He hated folding clothes. But it needed to be done, and he'd rather do it now. The cool thing was he didn't have to carry his clothes upstairs, since no one was here to lecture him on putting his clothes away.

Matt grabbed an armload of clothes from the dryer and carried them to the dining room table, where he dropped them in a heap. He went back for the rest and tossed it into the pile. For a moment, he considered just leaving his clothes in a disorganized heap on the table. If he weren't so finicky about wrinkles in his pants and shirts, he would have left them in disarray. Instead, he picked up a shirt and folded it. He stacked his shirts in a pile and placed his underwear and socks next to them. His jeans and jogging pants he set adjacent to the socks and underwear pile. As he was folding the last pair of jeans, he felt something inside the pocket. He frowned.

These were the jeans he'd worn Thursday night. Nothing should've been inside the pocket, since he hadn't put anything in there. Curious, he reached in and pulled out several torn pieces of paper. It seemed to be a sheet of notebook paper folded into a small rectangle. Pieces had torn off in the wash. A wave of nausea washed over him. He laid the pieces out on the table. There was writing on them, but most of it was indecipherable, faded from the water. The largest chunk of the sheet had formed itself into a clump that he could not pull apart. He threw out the useless pieces after examining them and was left with three small bits with legible writing on them.

Matt squinted, trying to read the words. The handwriting was not his own, and he did not recognize it. The note or whatever it was had been written in black ink. All he could make out from the remaining pieces were three words: god, son, and devil. A cold sweat slathered his brow. There were other words around these three words, but he could not read them. Shaking, he pushed the bits of paper away from him, stepped back from the table, and stood there, blinking. At last, he rushed up to his room. As he raced up the staircase, the three words from the scraps of paper invaded his mind. God, son, and devil, he thought.

The Runaround

Garrett paused when he was sure Matt could not see him. A macabre notion flashed through his mind. He held his breath, listening to the wind rattling through the tree leaves. When he let it out, a lump formed in his throat. What if someone was waiting for him to leave Matt alone? He surveyed the neighborhood. Although no one was around, his pulse quickened. The absence of an apparent threat made him quiver. Wheezy breaths struggled from his mouth. Sweat gleamed on his forehead. He wiped it away with his coat sleeve.

This is absurd, he decided and got moving again, increasing his pace. He had two miles to walk. Thankfully, the sun had melted the snow down quite a bit. But the gloomy shadows cast by the trees and bushes got to him. When he reached the busy highway at the end of Matt's street, a great weight departed from his chest.

The respite was brief. His chest hitched. He felt eyes boring into his back. Garrett chanced a peek over his shoulder. No one was there. The bright glare of headlights in his periphery gathered his attention. He studied the cars as they whizzed by. Their lights splashed across his view, invading the lonesome eve, and left their surreal glory frozen in his memory. He shivered in spite of his father's heavy coat. The traffic cleared, and he jogged across the highway.

For a while, he occupied his mind with thoughts of various games he wanted to play. As night devoured the sky, however, he fought to remain unaware of how secluded the streetlights looked. Passing between them was like entering a vast chasm in the earth. Each time he made it to the safety of a pool of light, intense gratitude filled him until he once more entered the shadows. He pulled the coat tighter around his shoulders and hunched against the wind. Halfway home, he let out a strangled breath. An odd notion had just snared him. *Matt and I thought that someone caused the snowstorm to isolate him, but what if its purpose was to protect him by keeping someone away from him? But who could have done it? I'll file this for later consideration,* he decided.

Garrett sidestepped a fallen tree branch and skirted around a patch of ice without pause. Soon, he came to a viaduct and followed the sidewalk upward. Below him were several sets of train tracks leading to the train station on his left. *This would be a good location for a movie,* he thought. *A movie about the rough and tumble 1930s or something. Yes, that could be a cool flick.* In his mind's eye, he replaced the train station with a speakeasy. The building he envisioned was red brick. A man clad in a black pinstripe suit and a snazzy fedora burst from the exit. On the man's lapel was a flower. Garrett expected a rose, but the flower was a yellow daisy. *How peculiar. That seems out of place,* he noted.

As he came down the other side of the viaduct, a jolt of unease lashed through his body. A sign now hung above the door to the speakeasy. In faded gold letters it read, BEYOND RESCUE ARE THOSE WHO ENTER HERE. His shoulders quaked. Glancing over his shoulder, he was sure he would see someone following, but he was alone. His shoulders drew up even further as he lowered his head.

I'm rather like a turtle right now, he realized. A laugh rose in his throat. As he scooted past the sign for Richard Street, it occurred to him that unlike a turtle, he had no shell to cover his back. Usually, he took Richard Street on the way home from Matt's, because it was a more direct route and shaved almost ten minutes from his walk. He had gone a different way today and had forgotten this street altogether until coming across it at this junction. Even from here, however, it would save a couple minutes.

Although anxious to get home, he was about to bypass it and go the longer way. He stopped in the middle of the road. That's just superstitious, he thought, turning down Richard Street. As he did, he almost clobbered a guy standing beside him. Where did he come from? Garrett gaped, noting that the young man, no older than his late twenties, was wearing a battered green army coat.

"Sorry, sir. I didn't mean to almost cream you," he apologized.

The young man ignored his comment and replied, "Can't you read the sign?"

"Um, what?"

The man pointed back toward the street sign. "Can't you read the sign?" he repeated.

"I beg your pardon, but I already know this is Richard Street."

The guy shook his head. "You need to read the sign before you go trespassing here."

"What? Trespassing? How am I trespassing?"

The man gazed at him without saying another word.

Garrett rolled his eyes and looked back at the street sign. If this guy wasn't a veteran, I'd—His jaw dropped. The sign no longer stated the street name. Instead, it proclaimed, REALM OF MONSTERS.

He whirled around. "What is this, some kind of—" he trailed off.

The man was gone. With everything that's happened, why am I surprised? He shook his head and looked over his shoulder again. Just an ordinary street sign now. Should have seen that coming. He considered venturing down the street anyway, in spite of these things. The only thing hindering him was a blatant observation of how few streetlights donned Richard Street. I'll just take Broadway to Monroe, he decided as he jogged away. Really wish I was a mixed martial arts fighter right now. If I was Eric Bradach, I wouldn't have to put up with this. Ghouls and government wackos, meet my fists. Yeah, that would be sweet.

Matt was so fidgety after he found the note that he dragged his laundry up and put it away just to get his mind off things. Now, he sat at the kitchen table with a pen in his hand. He was writing a short backstory for a video game that he and Garrett wanted to create. They were titling it *The Mystery of Hill Court*, for now anyway. Matt had named the house where the game took place. Garrett had chosen the protagonist's dopey name: Miller T. Missal.

"Miller T. Missal had heard the ghost stories about Hill Court all his life. In fact, back when it used to be a store called Hill Court Mini Mall (the bronze plaque still hung above the door), he had visited the store with his uncle. He'd been afraid of the old lady selling candy and other goods, thinking she was a witch and that her candy was poisoned. Shortly after that visit, the store had closed. A few weeks later, he had been playing near the house with friends. Their attention had been drawn by a barrel out in the driveway with something burning in it.

A black hearse was parked in the drive. He and his friends watched two men bring a body bag out of the house and carry it to the waiting hearse. Once he'd grown up and moved out of town, the memory nagged at him. Something about it struck him as wrong, and Hill Court beckoned him, no matter how far away he went. So he'd come back to Lostant, the town where he'd grown up. He called the realtor responsible for selling Hill Court. No one answered. For three days he'd gone to the office and gotten the runaround. Frustrated, he decided to sneak in and have a look around," he read.

It sounded cheesy when he said it out loud, but it was a start. Excited, Matt fetched some copy paper and sketched out the floor plans for the three story home. He wasn't very good at drawing, but he could make blueprints easily enough. Once he had done this, he sighed. He longed to see what the house would look like inside and out. I know, he thought, I'll have Jeff draw the design and an even better layout of the house. All I have to do is map out where I want the furniture, and I'll bet he could either draw it or create a model for me. He smirked. Wait until Garrett found out that he was going to enlist Jeff's help for their game. He'd go bananas.

Now maybe if I decide the color schemes, we could get Liz to make some concept art for us, he decided. Liz was Garrett's girlfriend, and she was always on board with whatever wild ideas they cooked up. Matt grabbed the phone and dialed Garrett's number.

"Kangley Mortuary. We specialize in cold cuts," Garrett answered.

"Hi, Gar," Matt greeted.

"Whatever is it, Matthew? I was just about to shower."

"Hey, I was thinking we could get Jeff to help design the house. Maybe he could make a model, too, and Liz could paint it."

"A model? Of whose house? Wait, why would Liz paint a house?"

"I meant the house for the game."

"Oh, so you want Jeffrey to design the thing? I thought you were working on that?"

"I did the floor plans, but you know I can't draw. So Jeff can draw the house from the floor plans and make a model of the rooms, and we could get Liz to paint the model or make some concept paintings for the interior of the house."

"I see. Well, Jeff would be a big help with that. And you know Liz is up for anything artistic."

Matt was so excited that he missed the tension in Garrett's voice. "Sweet. I've got the rough draft of the backstory complete."

"Bring it tomorrow, and we'll talk about it at lunch."

"All right, cool. Bye, man."

"Bye."

That's odd. He usually throws in some off the wall remark before hanging up, Matt thought.

Garrett's eyes fluttered open. He glanced at the clock. Four a.m.? He groaned. What a terrible time to have to use the bathroom, he thought, rolling out of bed. As he traversed the hall, a vision entered his mind. A tunnel filled with blackness that was even darker than the night which lay before him came into view. Outside the tunnel was a single streetlight illuminating the darkness. It looked safe outside the tunnel, but the inside teemed with danger. He could no longer focus on his surroundings, because the vision consumed him. He paused. I don't like the evil radiating from that tunnel, nor do I like the fact that I am seeing it in front of me, even though I'm still in the hallway.

"Walk inside the tunnel," a soft voice told him. He knew the voice was inside him, but he also knew that it was somehow separate from his thought-voices.

Garrett started. But the peaceful voice urged him onward. "Walk inside the tunnel," the voice insisted.

Will you be with me, he thought. He wasn't sure why, but he felt safe in the presence of the disembodied voice.

"Yes," answered the speaker.

Garrett stepped forward, shaking. Once he entered, he was immersed in blackness, and he found himself in the middle of the tunnel. He wasn't sure how he knew this was the center, but he was certain it was. At that moment, light emerged from inside him. The light funneled up through him and flooded the tunnel with white. He never got to see the inside of the tunnel. One moment it was pitch black; the next, he saw white rays piercing the darkness, and then he was enveloped in white. The tunnel and the abysmal blackness were no more. In that instant, he knew that the evil and the darkness were lies, an illusion thinner than a veil. At last, he was free of the vision, and he blinked, back in the hallway once more.

He walked into the bathroom and switched on the light. When he concluded his business, he hesitated. His eyes roamed over the light switch. Taking his time, he backed out of the room and leaned forward, stretching out his arm. As his fingers hit the switch, he held his breath. At last, his groping fingers managed to push the lever down. The bathroom light went off. He paused a moment, then whipped around and lit out for his room, running as fast as he could. Good thing Mom, Dad, and Milo have their rooms in the other wing, he thought. His parents would be angry about the noise he was making, and Milo would laugh at him. That was all he needed.

"Hey, Gar, did you understand what Mr. Brandenburg was talking about this morning?" Matt asked.

"Hm, I think he was blathering on about the War of 1812 or something. After that, it went right over my head."

"I know. He sure likes to bloviate, doesn't he?" Matt grinned.

"Ooh, I think I remember now. It was the Invasion of the Vorticons. Or was it the Americans? I always get the two confused."

"Isn't that an old Commander Keen game?"

"Hm. Circa early nineties? I believe it is. Though I can't imagine what the American forces were doing wasting their time with a frivolous game. Is it possible that I'm even more confused than I thought?"

"It's not only possible, it's probable."

Garrett mimicked him with a nasty glare.

Matt chuckled at him, and he rolled his eyes. "Geez, what's with you today? You're all snarky."

"I am not," Garrett answered.

"Yes, you are."

"Just show me the backstory for the game," he demanded.

"All right. Sorry."

Garrett sighed. "So what did you come up with?" Matt handed him the story sheet, and he read it over. "It's a bit hokey, but I think it'll do."

"Gee, thanks," Matt muttered.

"I said it would do. Should I have told you it would do nicely instead?"

"You made your point."

Garrett replied with a curt nod.

"Are you okay? You're very grumpy."

"I am rather grumpy, aren't I?" he said, nodding less curtly.

"Did something happen to you on the way home last night?" Matt whispered.

Garrett sucked in a sharp breath. How does he do that, he wondered. "Let's just say I had a rough night and leave it at that."

Matt's eyes widened. "What do you mean?"

"Never mind that. Nothing happened after I left, did it?"

"Yeah. I found this in with my laundry," he said and handed over the pieces of the note.

Garrett studied the torn pieces. "This isn't your handwriting. Weirdness just follows you around, doesn't it?"

Matt nodded. "What do you think it means?"

"I beg your pardon, sir, but I am not the bearer of answers."

Matt grinned.

"Well, well, a regular Sir Lancelot, huh?" interjected Jeff.

Garrett beamed at him. "Greetings, Jeffrey. Where is your fine friend Robert today?"

"Hey," griped Bobby as he approached the table, "that's even worse than being called Bob."

"Duly noted, Sir Bob."

Bobby raised his fist. Garrett shrank back, feigning terror. Jeff rolled his eyes. "You had to get him going, didn't you, Bobby."

"Whoa, back up, man. You started this one."

"So I did. Duly noted, Bob."

"One more person calls me Bob or Robert or Rob," he emphasized, glaring at Garrett as he opened his mouth, "and I will deck them."

Gar shut his mouth a second, then blurted out, "What if we call you Mr. Chickenpants?"

"Then it is with great pleasure that I shall melee you, M.O.M."

That quieted Garrett once and for all, though he wore a pouty face. Matt spoke up. "Jeff, I was wondering if you would help me with something for a video game that Gar and I are working on."

Jeff raised his eyebrows. "You need my help? Why?"

"Our game takes place in this house, but I can't draw and neither can Garrett. So I was thinking if you made sketches or a model of the house for us, we could have Liz design the interior."

Jeff rubbed his chin. "Hm. Yeah, I guess I could do that."

"Hey, what about me?" Bobby asked. "Don't I get to help?"

"What skills do you have that could be of use to us?" inquired Garrett.

"I can beta test the game for you when it's done and give feedback." Matt paused. "I'm cool with that if Garrett is."

Garrett nodded. "Fine. Oh, I meant to tell you, Mattie, that Liz definitely wants to work on this. It's right up her alley."

"Splendid."

Bobby, Jeff, and Garrett eyed him, craning and swiveling their necks to look at him from different positions.

"What?" Matt said.

"Who says splendid anymore other than corny movie villains?" Garrett said.

"Well, who says bloody, other than you and British people?" Matt returned.

"Mm, yes, I see your point, good sir," he replied with a pompous tone.

Matt opened his mouth to respond. His unuttered comment was dismissed by the clanging of the bell.

"See you chaps later," Garrett called as he bounded away for class.

Matt trudged off to fifth period. The remainder of the day passed quickly. Jeff and Bobby hitched a ride home with some older kids, leaving Matt to walk alone. He didn't mind. Garrett waved at him as he trotted by.

"Until tomorrow, Gar," Matt called.

Garrett stopped in mid-stride. "Aw, that's bloody adorable. Bye, bye, Matthew."

An unwanted grin stretched across Matt's lips. He waved. Garrett bowed in reply, making him laugh. "You look ridiculous," he yelled.

"You're just jealous that I am such a free spirit."

"Yeah, free to be weird."

"Hey," he chided, "I am a dork, so I can get away with acting uncool. What's your excuse? Besides, that's why you love me."

Matt groaned. *Why did I start with him?* "Fine. See ya."

"Adieu."

Matt had a little over a mile to walk. Heading south down the sidewalk along the Route 23, he noted that the snow was down to three inches. A breeze whipped up, throwing open his windbreaker. He smiled. Light breezes in the fall always made him feel excited, as if adventure were right around the corner. Would it be a pleasant one or one full of fright, he wondered, barely noticing the footsteps behind him. In his heart, he would have fancied nothing better than to have a grand adventure full of fun peppered with a modest amount of danger.

As Garrett crossed the highway, he mulled over how the player would navigate through the environment in their game, what objects would be needed, and how they fit into the story. He had several ideas for items that he wanted the character to grab during the gameplay, but he was stuck on the objective of the character. Other than the vague "explore the mystery house" theme, there seemed to be no goal. *We need to figure out the ending and work backward to find the purpose, mystery, and traps for this house,* he decided. Gradually, a wet crunching sound behind him registered on his radar. He did not turn around. Instead, he increased his pace little by little.

A few blocks from home, he crossed the intersection for Locust Street, willing the person behind him to go down that street. No such luck. Options ran through his head. *I could run and alert this person to my suspicion or calmly walk home. Or I could detour away from the house and backtrack. But if this person is following me, that might put me in further peril. On the other hand, if I go straight home, I risk the person finding out where I live.* It was quite the conundrum, and Garrett trod heavier upon the snow as he pondered.

The person encroached at a steady yet faster pace. Gar's heart thumped in his chest, urging him to make a break for it. He was on the verge of sprinting, when he was stopped by a singular query, which stuck in him like barbed wire. *What if this person already knows where I live?* An icy chill shuddered through his veins. He stopped, turning to face his stalker. About ten feet behind him stood a man of average height and medium build. His eyes were brown, and he had salt and pepper hair. He wore a charcoal suit with a burgundy tie and carried a black briefcase. Garrett had never seen him before.

"Sir, do you need directions or something?" he asked.

The man frowned. "What?"

"I presume that you are a traveling salesman. Am I correct?"

"How did you know that?" the man quizzed, narrowing his eyes.

"The suit and the briefcase give you away, I'm afraid."

"Oh. Oh my, yes," the man replied, mopping sweat off his brow with his forearm. Afterward, he ran a hand through his hair.

"Are you lost?"

"No. I'm on my way to Richard Street," he explained, shifting his eyes away.

Garrett didn't buy it. *I'll just bet you are*, he thought. *You're lying, good sir. My bet is that you're headed for Monroe Street to spy on me.* "Oh," he replied, "so what's your name? And what are you selling?"

"Uh, my name is Phillip Downey. I'm selling eco-friendly cleaners."

"Poor Mr. Downey. I wish you luck. That's a tough sell at any time, especially the fall."

Mr. Downey laughed. A nervous edge crept into his voice. "You'd think it was winter, with all this snow on the ground. It leaves too many tracks."

Garrett furrowed his brow, his nerve endings screaming. The hair on his neck and arms stood up. "Pardon? What do you mean by that?"

Mr. Downey's eyes widened. "I, er, just meant that the snow tracks up everything. It gets all over the mats in my car and makes a mess."

"I see. I recommend Weathertech floor mats. My Dad finds them a huge help, worth the price. Well, good luck, Mr. Downey."

"Thanks, boy." The man paused, and when Garrett didn't move or even turn around, he jogged past, waving as he did so.

But Garrett could see frustration come over him as he hurried off. He watched Mr. Downey gain some distance, cross the road, and turn left down Everett Street, a block before Monroe. Meanwhile, Garrett stood in a rigid posture, with his hand on his chin and his head tilted up. Once the salesman was out of sight, he raced home. *I knew that guy was lying. If he was really going to Richard Street, he would have gone right on Everett.*

When he was left with just a quarter mile to go, Matt abruptly became attuned to his surroundings. Again, he registered footsteps behind him. He glanced to his right. No one was around. Usually, there were a bunch of kids from the junior high laughing and jumping about as they wandered home. He looked over at the highway as he passed the police station. There was no traffic. He hadn't seen much over the past fifteen minutes, which was strange for a busy time of day. The emptiness around him made his heartbeat increase a little. And still those footsteps crunched along behind him.

How long had he heard them? Nearly the whole way now, he realized. Matt cringed. He had come past downtown into the residential area. There were no businesses nearby, save for BG's Breads. And most people were not even home from work yet. His head pounded.

He stopped for a moment and readjusted the strap of his backpack with trembling fingers. He could hear the person behind him getting closer. At last, Matt decided what he would do. He slowed his pace to a saunter, hoping the person would pass him. To his dismay, the footsteps behind him dwindled to a dawdle. Now what, he wondered. He kept going, about to come unglued, until he reached his street corner. A few cars darted by on the highway, and the footsteps paused for a moment.

Once he turned the corner of Waterford, he crossed the street, whirled around, and walked backwards up the sidewalk. Edging ever closer to the house, he kept his eyes trained on the end of the road. A man stepped into view. He was short with wavy, brown hair and gray eyes. He wore a green suit with a bright red tie and shiny, black loafers that appeared two-toned because of white spats.

There was something familiar about him, but Matt couldn't put his finger on it. His face was young. He looked to be in his early thirties. In his right hand was a dark red handkerchief. A couple of drops of liquid dripped off the end of it onto the ground as he glanced up the street. When he saw Matt staring back at him, his eyes widened. He turned and fled down 23, continuing in the same direction he'd been going. If Garrett had been with him, Matt might have chased after the fellow.

Whipping around, he dashed home and hurried inside, locking the door behind him. In the kitchen, he peered out through one of the blinds. He did not see the man anywhere down by the highway. Heart pounding, he went to look out front. No, the guy wasn't creeping up the street, either. *If he was following me, why was he dressed so conspicuously?* It dawned on him that the guy may have meant to harm him. He shook his head, refusing to consider what this might mean.

The Fire of Resistance

MATT PICKED UP the phone and paused. No, he decided. I can't run to Gar every time something happens. He put the phone back in its holder and turned his mind instead to the mystery of what Mr. Brandenburg had been talking about in class that morning. He rifled through his backpack for his History book, groaning as he opened up the text. Ugh, why did Brandenburg give us so much homework?

Garrett entered the house, thankful that his Mom hadn't returned from picking up Milo yet. His father was still at work. Panting, he went to the fridge and grabbed a soda. He took a huge swig, dribbling a bit down the front of his shirt. Immediately, he began coughing. He pounded his chest. When he finished hacking, he retreated to his room. He would be alone for a few minutes yet, so he was going to record a video game playthrough with his camera, adding his own commentary with a microphone. First he set up the camera, next he readied the microphone. That done, he grabbed an old favorite from his shelf, wishing he had time to record more than just one level.

Finished at last, Matt thought, shoving his books and notebooks back into his book bag. He glanced at the clock on the oven. It was already four-thirty. His gaze slid over to the blinds covering the sliding door. He opened the blinds a little ways and looked out. No one was lurking outside. He glanced at the lock. Still engaged. Good, he thought and shut the blinds. As he shifted in the chair, his eyes fell on the basement door. After some consideration, he got up. He paused, hand on the knob. His palms perspired, and when he tried to turn the knob, they slipped off the handle.

Scowling, he wiped his hands on his jeans and yanked the door open. His heart knocked against his ribs. All was as it should be. He let out a pent-up breath. He'd half-expected the stalker to be waiting for him on the landing. As he went down, he saw that the door was locked, deadbolt still engaged. He turned, leaping up the last two steps and throwing the door shut behind him. It banged closed, shaking the doorframe. Matt stifled a yell. Once his heart stopped racing, he fetched his phone. He called Jeff, but Jeff was busy. Bobby also had plans.

"Sorry, Matt. I can't come over tonight. I promised the Bakers that I'd watch a movie with them, and they'll be here any minute."

"What are you guys gonna watch?" he asked.

"Something called *Revenge for the Wicked*."

"You're seriously gonna watch that?" He snickered.

"What's so funny?" Bobby demanded.

"Bobby, you know that's a chick flick, right?"

"It is? I thought—I mean, the title makes it sound like a horror movie."

"Nope. I've seen the ads for that on Youtube. It's definitely a chick flick."

"Aw, man. This sucks."

"Have fun watching your chick movie," Matt teased.

"Hey, at least I'll be hanging out with some girls."

"Just don't act like one," he countered.

"That's low, dude."
"Bye."
"Bye. Creep."
Matt hung up.

A huffy grunt issued from Garrett's throat. He slammed his History book shut. No more homework. That evil Brandenburg is trying to kill us all, I swear, he thought. Pft, History, what a useless subject. That wasn't really how he felt, of course. He merely liked to vent his dislike of Mr. Brandenburg's teaching style on the subject. His thoughts rattled on until it occurred to him that Milo had yet to barge in on him. Perhaps he's still not feeling well, although he made it through school today. I should probably check on him—or not. Uttering something unintelligible, he lifted himself off the bed and sashayed down to the other wing of the house. Milo's door was closed. Very unusual. Normally, he would have taken this opportunity to throw the door open with reckless abandon, thereby returning the favor to Milo, but tonight, he knocked.

He heard a cough then Milo grumbled, "What do you want?"

Garrett opened the door to see his brother in bed. His face was pale, though his cheeks were red. Startled, Garrett said, "Milo, let me check your forehead."

Milo shrank back from him. "No. I want Mom."

"I'll get her in a minute. But I came to see if you're feeling better."

Milo shook his head. Garrett put his hand on the boy's forehead. He was burning up. "I'm going to get Mom. You've got a fever."

"Okay," Milo said, ending his sentence with a heart-wrenching hack.

Garrett ran to the living room, where his parents were watching television. "Hey, um, has Milo taken any medicine recently? Because I just checked on him, and he's burning up."

"He is? I thought you were gonna take him back to the doctor?" his father said to his mother.

"Brandon, I couldn't get him in today. Anyway, he seemed so much better this morning that I let him go to school. He was fine when he came home. Come on, let's see if he's all right."

His dad shut the TV off, and they went to look in on Milo. Garrett headed into the kitchen for something to drink. He got a glass out of the cabinet, took the tea pitcher out of the fridge, and poured himself a glass. Then he sat at the table, lost in thought.

When his mother wandered in, he looked up and said, "Is he okay?"

"Well, he's sleeping now. But we gave him his medicine before he went out. I don't think he's gonna make it to school tomorrow, though," she replied.

"Aw," Garrett said.

He followed her into the den. She turned on the radio.

"What are you listening to?"

"The local station."

"I see. I didn't even know you listened to the radio."

"Don't get smart with me, Garrett."

"I wasn't implying anything. I just meant I've never seen you listen to it, is all."

She smirked at him. "Sure, sure. And you're not implying that I'm old, then, are you?"

Garrett hid a guilty smile. Man, she was good.

"That's what I thought," she said. "I'll bet you were gonna add, 'Geez, Mom, I didn't even know you knew what a radio was,' weren't you?" she asked, imitating his voice quite well.

"Actually, I was going to ask if radios even existed in your day," he joked.

She raised her eyebrows, saying nothing.

"Okay, guilty. So what are you listening to? Would it by any chance be the Golden Oldies station?"

"Enough mouth, mister. I'm trying to catch the forecast. Someone texted me earlier saying there's a chance another snowstorm is headed our way."

"Why not look it up on your phone?" he asked.

"I can't stand looking things up like that. I don't trust those weather apps," she explained.

"Then why not just turn on the news and watch the weather report?"

"Too many images. It's just too busy for my taste."

"I see. So even adults don't like watching the news?"

"Nope."

"Then why do you do it?" he inquired.

"Because it's our responsibility to know what's going on, that's why."

"Makes sense."

They were silent for a moment as the news report came on. Garrett was only half listening. That is, until he heard: "In other news, a peculiar discovery was made in a dumpster in the neighboring town of Ransom. It seems a Ransom resident was taking out the trash for Stanley's Bar, when he came upon something shocking. Inside the dumpster was what at first appeared to be a dead German shepherd. Upon further investigation, it turned out to be a life-sized, stuffed replica covered in some sort of syrup. The man has no idea how it got there, but he believes it to be a prank by some would-be vandals. Talk about taxidermy gone awry, folks. Coming up, your hourly weather report."

Garrett's eyes went wide. He stumbled and almost fell over. His head pounded.

"Garrett? You all right? Please tell me you're not getting sick too," his mom cried, placing her hand on his forehead. She shut the radio off with her other hand.

"I—" He coughed. The alarm on her face tore at his heart. "I'm fine, Mom. It's just vertigo, is all."

"Are you sure?" she asked.

"Yes."

She continued to examine him. "You seem fine, but I want you to go to bed early tonight and get some rest."

"Okay," he managed.

His father appeared in the doorway. "What's going on?"

"Nothing. Garrett has vertigo, and I was worried he might be getting pneumonia," she explained.

His father stared hard at him. "You be sure to wear my heavy coat to school as whenever it gets too cold. We don't need you getting sick like Milo."

Garrett nodded.

He narrowed his eyes. "Are you sure you're feeling well? You're awfully pale."

"I'm fine. Really."

"Let me know if you start feeling ill."

"Sure, Dad." When he left, Garrett said, "Mom, would it be okay if I went to Matt's after school tomorrow?"

She was quiet, considering his request. "Well, all right. If you're certain you're not getting sick."

"Nope, right as rain."

"Fine. I'll pick you two up and drop you off on the way to the doctor's."

"Thanks, Mom."

She smiled at him. "You going to bed now?"

He started to protest, it being only 8:00, two hours before his usual bedtime, but then he remembered that he'd said he would go to sleep early. "Absolutely, Mother dear," he replied.

She chuckled as he went out the door. Garrett returned to his room. He left the lights off in case his parents ventured by. Instead of going to bed, however, he turned on the computer and searched the internet for information about the dumpster dog found in Ransom. He found nothing about the incident. Sighing, he moved the cursor to close out the browser then paused. Just for the heck of it, he thought. He typed Norm Morriston's name into the search box and hit enter. Scrolling through the few relevant hits, he found the official webpage for the politician.

Matt never told me the guy actually has his own site. He clicked on it and read through the information. *Boy, this doesn't tell me* anything useful at all. But at least now he knew what the man looked like. A handsome, young politician beamed at him from the homepage. Yet Garrett frowned as he looked at the smiling image. Even in just a photo, he found Matt's description of the guy's eyes to be accurate. *I've never seen such malicious eyes,* he thought.

He went to exit the browser when he spotted a brief promo video on the page featuring Morriston. Shrugging, he clicked on it.

"Hello, friends and constituents of the 7th district," said Norm Morriston, an air of implied magnanimity in his voice. "Norm Morriston here. When you consider your choices this November, I hope you will examine my record carefully. We can't give up hope, and we can't wait: America needs your help for recovery. Remember, I side with the little guy, with Main Street, not Wall Street. Thank you for taking the time to visit my website. I hope to have earned your trust and your vote."

Even his voice oozes insincerity and arrogance, Garrett noted. He shuddered as he closed the browser and shut down the computer.

The following morning, Matt sat in the computer lab before first period, putting the final touches on an English essay. He found it hard to concentrate and glanced at the seat beside him, occupied by Jeff. Jeff was glaring at the computer screen and making frustrated noises. More than once, he looked as if he would pick up the wireless mouse and launch it across the room.

"Come on. I just did that," he growled. "C'mon. Autocad draw line. What is wrong with this thing? Gah."

Matt cast a surreptitious glance at Mr. Pierce, the lab monitor. Fortunately, he had his back to them, employed on the other side of the room. Matt shifted his gaze back to Jeff. "Dude, calm down before Mr. Pierce hears you."

Jeff ignored him. "You're so great at hand-drafting. You should take computer drafting. You'd be a natural, they said. This stupid program," he muttered.

"Relax, bro."

"Matt, if you ever want me to do a digital model of that house for you, I have to learn to use this program. Besides, all you're doing is writing an essay. That's nothing compared to this."

"I don't get it. You're good at all those computer drawing and animation programs. Why is this so hard for you?"

"Probably because I don't know computer language. I'll get it figured out. That's why I'm putting in extra practice."

"It's not worth getting so worked up over."

"It is if you want to be an architect, which I do. Remember?"

"Well, since you agreed to help me and Garrett with the game, I could have Garrett ask Liz to get her brother Randy to help you. You know he's awesome at this."

"That would be great. Cuz, man, I hate Autocad."

After school, Garrett met him outside. "Matt, I'm coming over. Mom's gonna give us a ride to your house."

"You're coming over? Why?" Matt asked.

"I'll tell you when we get there."

"Fine. Why's your mom giving us a ride?"

"She has to take Milo to the doctor."

"Is he all right? I thought he went to school yesterday?"

"He did, but last night his fever returned."

"Oh. I hope he gets better soon."

"As do I, Mattie."

Bobby and Jeff suddenly appeared. "You coming, bro?"

"Sorry, Bob, but Gar and I are hitching a ride with his mom today."

"That's cold, dude."

"Gets you back for yesterday."

"Hey, Garrett," Jeff interjected. "Listen, thanks for having Liz talk to Randy during lunch. He said he'd help me."

"No problem, Jeffrey. Oh, look, here's our ride. Ta-ta, gentlemen."

"See you guys," Matt called. When he got into the car, he said, "Hi, Mrs. Lee. Thanks for the ride."

"You're welcome, Matt."

"Hey, Milo, buddy. Get well soon, okay?"

Milo coughed. "Thanks, Matt."

Garrett's mom dropped them off a few minutes later. Before she left, she called, "Garrett. Your father will pick you up at seven. I don't want you walking home, even if it's not going to snow."

"Okay, Mom. See you later."

"Bye, sweetie. I love you."

Garrett blushed. "Love you too, Ma."

She drove off. Matt smirked, ribbing him. "Aw, somebody loves our little Master of Melee."

"Knock it off, Matt. We have much to discuss."

"Cut the drama and just tell me what's going on."

"Not out here," he replied with a furtive glance about.

"Let's go in, then."

Garrett followed him to the kitchen. Matt opened the fridge and took out two sodas. Sitting at the table, he shoved the other can of soda toward Garrett, who took it but did not open it.

"All right, spill it, Gar."

"Matthew, as you know, I am your loyal friend," he began.

Matt groaned and hung his head in his hands. "I knew this was gonna be bad news."

"I'm sorry, Mattie."

"Get to the point."

"Fair enough. Last night, Mumsy and I were listening to the radio, when there came a news report. Naturally, I wished to run and hide, but as there was nowhere to go, I simply submitted to the arcane torture. And what do you think I heard?"

Matt tensed up. His throat constricted. "Norm Morriston," he guessed.

"Nope. What I heard was a report about a man taking out the trash outside Stanley's Bar in Ransom." He paused for effect.

"That's all? Why should I care about that?"

"Because the man found what he thought was a dead dog in the dumpster."

A chill ran through him. "You mean—"

Garrett nodded. "Yes. He soon realized it was a stuffed replica, covered in syrup, assumed to be the work of vandals. It doesn't sound as though he investigated it closely enough to notice that the beast was not merely stuffed with cotton. I tried to find more info on the web, but I came up empty-handed. However, just for giggles, I looked up this Mr. Morriston. He is every bit as creepy as you described. I bow to your descriptive prowess."

"You did? Did you find his website, then?"

"I did indeed. Vague, vapid, and revealing nothing."

"Yep. Typical political spiel."

"There's more."

"Uh-oh. I don't like the sound of that."

"Yesterday," he began in a raspy voice, "as I wandered home from prison,—I mean school—I was followed by a man purporting to be a traveling salesman. And he said something rather creepy."

"You were followed too?" Matt gawked.

"Wait, you too? Why on bloody earth didn't you tell me?" Garrett demanded.

"I could ask you the same thing."

"All right, all right. Never mind the secrecy. Do tell me of your experience."

"You first," he insisted.

Garrett stared at him.

"Hey, you started first," Matt reminded.

"So I did. Fair enough. This good gent had the audacity to follow me and then seem unnerved when I confronted him. I asked him if he was lost. He said he was looking for Richard Street, which I totally didn't buy. Then he said something about not liking the snow because it leaves too many tracks. When I asked what he said, he covered his tail by remarking that snow tracks up his car too badly when he gets in it. Anyway, then he waited for me to keep going, but I stayed put until he walked off ahead of me. He turned left down Everett Street, which is the wrong way if he was going to Richard Street. Anyway, then I vamoosed."

"Wow, that's freaky. What was he supposed to be selling?"

Garrett laughed and said, "Get this, he said he selling green cleaning products."

Matt laughed. "No way."

"I swear on my love of video games."

"Bizarre."

"So who followed you?"

"I noticed someone following me on the way home, but I was afraid to turn around. I slowed down, hoping the person would pass me. Instead, the person also slowed. So when I got to the end of my street, I turned the corner and started walking backward up the road. The man who was following me stepped into view, wearing this conspicuous green suit and red tie and these snazzy black loafers with those white things that go over them. What do you call them?"

"Spats?"

"Yeah, that's it. Why are they called spats, anyway?"

"It's short for spatterdash. They go over your shoes to protect them from dirt and mud."

"How do you know that, anyway?"

"Because it's my business to know such things, good sir," Garrett stated.

"Right. Anyway, so when the guy sees I'm watching him, he freaks out and runs down 23."

"Ye have an enemy, Matthew."

"Nay, we have an enemy."

Garrett shook his head. "Crazy."

"Gar," Matt asked, "why did you act so weird at lunch yesterday?"

He blanched. Man, sometimes it really freaks me out how he does that, Garrett thought. "If you must know," he said, adopting an air of bravado, "something occurred on my way home from your house Sunday evening."

"What?"

He decided he would tell Matt only about what happened on Richard Street and not about the middle of the night vision on his sojourn to the bathroom. "As I was trying to go down Richard

Street, I turned and nearly plowed a guy in an army coat. He goes, 'Can't you read the sign?' And I was all, 'I know I'm on Richard Street.' So he shakes his head and repeats, 'Can't you read the sign?' So I turn around to point out that we are indeed on Richard Street, only now the sign reads, 'Realm of monsters.' I was all like, 'Is this some sort of joke?' And when I turned back around, the dude was gone. So I looked at the sign again, and it was normal. Then I pretty much dashed home like a scared bunny. Meh."

"That is so out there."

"I know. But it's still not as bad as your house."

Matt raised his eyebrows but added, "That's definitely an understatement."

"Agreed."

"Wait a minute. Something just occurred to me."

"Pray tell, Matthew."

"You had a weird experience on Richard Street. Then the next day, that salesman tried to cover his tail by saying he was looking for Richard Street. Do you think there's a connection? It seems way too convenient to be a coincidence."

Garrett's jaw dropped. "You—I—how could—" he began. "Ahem," he continued, "I am an idiot. Thank you for pointing out my not-smartness."

"You're welcome," Matt returned, smirking.

With a toothy grin, he replied, "I approve of this mockery. The Master of Melee has taught you well."

"Get to the point."

"I'm bloody trying to. As I was gonna say before being rudely interrupted, this implies or confirms a theory I had."

"Oh?"

"When I realized I was being followed, a number of scenarios came to mind. One of them caused me to confront the salesman. I posited that he might already know whereabouts I live."

Matt gaped at him. "What?"

Nodding, he added, "Yes. And it very well might be true. He may have been observing me when I left Sunday night. If he saw what happened to me on Richard Street, it's likely that he had a slip of the tongue when I questioned him, as he did with the bit about the snow leaving tracks. Besides, I know he wasn't looking for Richard Street, because, as I mentioned earlier, when he ducked down Everett, he went the wrong way."

"Doesn't that suggest that he didn't know where Richard Street was?"

"It could, but if he was just using that as a cover and panicked, he might have gone the wrong way thinking he'd divert my suspicions. He did seem pretty inept. Also, if he had not observed my experience on Richard Street the night before, then why even mention Richard Street? Unless he really was just a traveling salesman, which I highly doubt."

"Then everything could just be a huge misunderstanding."

"Matt, he was not a bloody salesman. He waited for me to continue, and when it became obvious that I wasn't budging, he continued past me. If he was a real salesman, he would have tried to sell me something or asked me if I knew anyone in the area who could use his product. Trust me, it was a ruse."

Cringing, Matt said, "If that's the case, what can we do?"

"I don't know. Not yet, anyway." He paused, thinking.

Matt let loose a heavy sigh. *This is starting to get tedious,* he thought. After several minutes of silence passed, he looked up. Garrett remained pensive.

"Earth to Gar. Are you okay?"

"Hm? What?"

"I asked if you're all right."

"Yes, quite. I do have a question, though."

"Yeah?"

"You said that the guy following you was familiar somehow. What did he look like?"

"Short. Wavy, brown hair, gray eyes."

"Gray eyes? Norm Morriston has gray eyes."

"It couldn't have been him. I didn't pay much attention to his features, but if it was Morriston, then why would he dress so loudly?"

"Sometimes the greatest disguise is one that draws attention to you. Plus, inexperience mixed with arrogance makes people do strange things," he remarked.

"Yeah, that's not a creepy statement, no way."

"Sarcasm? I quite like that, Mattie."

"What's our next move?"

"I wish I knew. Kinda makes me glad that my dad is picking me up, though."

Matt blew out a noisy breath. "So what do you wanna do now?"

"What I want to do right now is River Dance. If only I had some tap shoes."

"You don't use tap shoes for River dancing."

"Maybe you don't. I will do whatever I want, thank you. Always good to mix it up."

"Why don't we watch a movie? I don't have the drive for video games right now."

"Psh, no drive, no ambition: that's so you. What movie?"

"I dunno. You pick."

"Ooh, delightful. I get to pick. *Bambi*?" he suggested.

"Um, no."

"Ugh, fine. Something macho, then. How about *Zombieland*?"

"Sure. I like that well enough."

"It's got zombies and humor. The perfect combination."

They settled down in the family room. Matt sat on the couch, flabbergasted. Garrett didn't speak the entire way through the movie. *I think that's the longest I've ever seen him be quiet*, Matt thought. *Voluntarily*, he amended. Not even in his sleep was Garrett so closed-mouthed. When the movie ended, Matt suggested they get their homework done. His suggestion was met with a groan.

"Gah, you are too neurotic, Matt."

"Don't you mean OCD?"

"Anal retentive," corrected Garrett.

"Whatever. Can we just get this done?"

"Fine. You do your schoolwork, and I shall play games."

"Focus, Garrett."

Pouting, he said, "You're really gonna make me do my homework right now? That's mean."

"Fine. Just go do whatever, but let me get mine done."

"Aw gee, thanks, Mom," he teased. Then he grabbed his backpack. "Thought you were gonna play games?"

"As a natural procrastinator, that is my wish. You're lucky I'm a loyal friend who will stand with you through the trials of homework," he murmured.

"Yes, I am." Matt smiled at him.

"Cute smile, Matt, but it's still not worth me doing my homework," he mused. Still, he appeased Matt by taking on the wretched task.

An hour later, they finished. *Wow, so Mr. Brandenburg being ill today really did lessen our workload.* Matt laughed at this thought.

"What's so funny?"

"I just realized that Brandenburg being sick made our homework load lessen substantially."

"Yes. At least his sub is a human being. One who's not trying to kill us all. Well, presumably."

Grinning, Matt said, "Now we can play games."

"Your drive has returned, eh? Calling it," he yelled as he raced upstairs for the PlayStation.

"Okay, but no Soul Reaper."

"Deal."

At six forty-five, they meandered out onto the porch to wait for Gar's father. While Garrett was making a mental itinerary for the remainder of his free time, Matt drank in the crisp air, attention absorbed in the patches of dwindling snow. Soon it would be gone. Sadness welled up inside him. He wasn't sure why, given that winter was on its way and would bring more snow. He turned to ask Garrett something and noticed that he was far away, a dreamy expression on his face. *I'll ask him about that tomorrow,* he decided. As his gaze fell on the snow again, a voice interrupted his thoughts.

"The fire of resistance burns in your soul," a wise voice told him.

Matt started and looked around, though he was pretty sure the voice was in his mind. He and Garrett were alone. *What does that mean? The fire of resistance?* He shook the thought away. Garrett remained oblivious.

Generations

GARRETT'S FATHER ROLLED down the window when he pulled up and said, "Hi, Matt. How are you doing?"

"I'm doing alright, Mr. Lee."

"That's good. Parents away again?"

Matt nodded.

"Must be lonely with them traveling so much."

"Well, at least this time it was for vacation and not business."

"Why didn't they wait until summer and take you?"

"This was the only time they were both free at the same time."

"I see. Are you ready to go, Garrett?"

"Yes. How's Milo?"

"They put him on some heavy duty medication, but the doctor thinks he'll be able to return to school in a few days."

"Good. Well, ta-ta, Matthew," Garrett called.

"See ya, man."

Matt watched him get into the car, raising a hand in farewell. Garrett grinned and waved back. When the car turned onto 23, Matt retreated into the house, locking the door behind him. Sighing, he took two boxes of Hamburger Helper Stroganoff out of the pantry and began preparing it. He couldn't eat even one box alone, but by making both boxes, he'd have food for a couple of days. He loathed cooking. Garrett was the opposite. Whenever Matt's parents were on one of their business trips, if Gar spent the night, he cooked for them. Matt had to admit, he was a good cook. Last Saturday, he hadn't asked Gar to make dinner because neither wanted Bobby and Jeff to know this. They would just rag on him.

When the stroganoff was done, he fixed a small plate. After supper, he put the leftovers in two plastic containers and stuck them in the refrigerator. By the time he got everything cleaned up, it was 8:30. I could mess around on my keyboard for a bit; see if I can come up with some theme music for the game, he decided.

He retrieved the keyboard, music stand, and a manuscript pad. As he set everything up, he recalled that Liz's older brother Randy played guitar. I should see if he wants to help with the music. Tinkering around on the keys, he found the beginning notes of a melody for the main theme. He wrote them down on the pad. All told, he completed eight bars, a small start but a start nonetheless. Stuck, he pushed the keyboard away and glanced at his watch. A yelp escaped him. It was 11:00. Better get to bed, he decided.

Garrett rushed through the kitchen doorway and collided with his dad.

"Sorry, Dad."

"That's all right. You're on your own for dinner. We already ate."

"That's fine."

After parting company with his father, he made two cold turkey sandwiches. Once he ate and cleaned up, it occurred to him that he should say hi to Milo. Milo did not respond to his soft knocks, and he was about to open the door, when his father spoke up from behind.

"He's asleep."

"Oh. I just wanted to say hello."

His dad nodded. "He'll be fine. Why don't you go finish your homework?"

"Already done. It was done before we left Matt's."

"Wow. Matt's a good influence on you."

"That he is, Father. But I always get my homework done one way or another, with or without Matthew's prodding."

"Yeah, right before bed, you procrastinator. Run along and go play your video games." He smiled.

Garrett gawked at him. "Who says run along to a fifteen-year-old?"

"I do. Go."

"Yes, sir."

He hurried to his room, deciding to download the remaining programs that were needed to go along with a program he'd recently downloaded called XNA Framework. He turned on the computer, eager and anxious. XNA Framework would allow him and Matt to create games. In order to use the framework, however, he needed to know a computer language called C#, which he didn't. Maybe he could pick it up with a little practice. When he finally got the programs installed, he spent the remainder of his time trying to fiddle with XNA. At last, he gave up, thinking, I shall have to go to the XNA forums. I'm sure there are tutorials for this thing. Or he could always buy books on the C# language. Good heavens, he mused, am I really considering reading non-school books? Perhaps I have got a touch of pneumonia. I shall call it Milo's Pneumonia of the Mind, or Milomonia. Vaccine forthcoming. Available soon from your local pharmacy.

Late that night, Matt awoke shivering and panting from a dream that seemed to be of great importance. Unfortunately, he could not remember the details. All he knew was that something was coming, something big and eminent. It's bad, he thought. Whatever it is, it's bad. Although groggy, he was alert enough to note the time. He stared at the red numbers on his alarm clock. It was 3:12 in the morning. He caught his breath and settled down. For a long while, his mind was blank.

Norm Morriston's face paraded out of the nothingness, plundering his attention. The wrathful eyes glared at Matt. Even in memory, it unhinged him. His heart tried to leap from his chest. What is this guy's goal, he wondered.

From a sheltered corner of his mind, he discovered another thought-voice, which spoke up from the gloom.

"You already know," this part of him proclaimed. And Matt fancied that he did know, but he refused to put it into words. "World domination," the other voice said.

Oh come on, Matt replied inwardly, do you know how cliché and paranoid that is?

The deep voice challenged, "And what do you think life will be like for Milo if this guy's power grab isn't stopped?"

Matt's eyes widened. Milo? This next generation could be in real trouble, he realized. Although he had no concrete proof yet, the idea felt more than logical: it felt sane, certain, and true. And it was plausible, because the country was in ever-worsening economic and political turmoil. Milo and those younger than himself would need good leaders and teachers.

Well, what can I do? I'm in trouble too, Matt thought. It was then that he remembered what this deep voice had told him when he was on the porch.

"The fire of resistance burns in your soul," that voice repeated.

I don't know what to do, Matt argued.

"You will. Just be who you are and leave the rest to me," the fading voice replied. This silenced his protests, but he couldn't help wondering where inside him that voice came from.

Garrett saw a fire burning. He knew he was asleep. But this seemed significant somehow. He looked around and discovered that he was in his own backyard. Milo and his parents were standing on his right, close to the flames, but no one was doing anything to stop the fire. He grabbed the nearest thing to him—a rake—and ran forward, beating at the flames. Why isn't anyone helping me, he wondered. Suddenly, a figure was standing to his left, beyond the fire. Gasping, he realized that the man before him was the soldier he'd met on Richard Street. The man was grinning at him.

"Sir, who are you?" Garrett called.

The man did not respond, just continued beaming at Garrett. He exuded an aura of pride. The source of this pride seemed to revolve around Garrett. Before Gar could ask more questions or put out the fire, he woke up and looked at the clock. It was 3:13 a.m. He jumped out of bed and left his room. When he got to Milo's room, he slipped in, closing the door behind him. The boy seemed to be in a peaceful sleep. His breath came out in ragged snorts. Garrett stood at his bedside, placing a hand on his forehead. Milo wasn't feverish. In fact, his skin was cool to the touch, a little clammy. Milo, get better soon, he thought. A new and urgent unease descended over him. He'd never felt so protective of the little guy. There was a connection here now that hadn't been there before. It was deeper than familial bond. Somehow, it was as if he'd tapped into Milo's future and seen something horrible lying in wait, a trap of some sort.

He caressed Milo's face. "I'm gonna do my best to protect you, Milomonia inspirer," he whispered.

He stood peering at his brother for a long time. At last, he left the room, his heart wrenched with love and fear. What am I trying to watch out for? This attack of nurturing instinct is worrisome. I guess M.O.M. is a fitting nickname, he mused.

The next day at lunch, Garrett strutted up to his girlfriend's table. "Liz, I need a favor."

"What?"

"Talk to Randy and see if he can help me learn C Sharp," he pleaded.

"Why don't you just ask him yourself?" Liz said.

"Because I'm afraid he'll be mad, since we already asked him to help Jeff with Autocad. Also, he thinks I'm weird."

"You are weird. It's your defining characteristic," she replied.

"It's also the source of my charm," he added.

"There is that."

"So will you ask him?" He looked at her with a puppy dog face.

"Oh, all right. Enough with the face."

"I'm lucky you love me."

"Yes, you are. But I lucked out in return, so I can't complain too much."

Garrett grinned. Liz responded with a helpless smile. What a kook he was. He put his arm around her. Nice and cuddly, he thought. His reverie was soon interrupted.

"Randy," Liz yelled when she saw him enter the lunchroom.

Tall and intimidating, he shouted back as he walked toward them, "What do you want?"

"Garrett needs your help with something."

Randy pointed at him. "Why can't you just ask me yourself, freak?"

"Because you're scary."

Randy rolled his eyes. "So what do you need help with now?"

"In my defense, I did not need help previously. I had Liz ask you on behalf of Jeff. Currently, I'm requesting your assistance in learning the C Sharp computer language."

"C Sharp? Why do you want to know that?" Before Garrett could answer, Randy said, "Of course. You're a gamer, but you want to develop."

Garrett nodded.

"I'm guessing you're gonna use XNA, right?"

"Yes."

"Fine. But it'll have to wait until Christmas break. If you want Jeff to pass his Cad program, that is."

"Deal. Thanks, dude."

"You guys are just lucky I'm so nice. One more thing. Liz, you owe me big for this."

"Fine. What do you want?"

"I want your solemn vow that you will never marry this wacko."

Liz smirked. "Done."

Garrett eyed her with huge, wounded eyes. When Randy was gone, she told him, "Relax. By the time we get married, he'll probably have grown up some."

"And if he hasn't?"

"Then I guess I just lied." She kissed his cheek.

"But, technically, didn't you just lie either way?"

"I might not have, if you keep correcting me," she admonished.

"Point taken."

After school, Garrett slung his backpack over his shoulder and walked out the door. Matt had already left. As he came outside, he saw his mother's car waiting for him. She honked at him.

"Hi, Mom," he said.

"Hop in. Your father and I got home early. He asked me to come get you and Matt."

"Matt already left."

"We'll pick him up."

"Okay. Is anything wrong?"

"We both thought Matt could use some company with his parents gone and everything. Besides, I was hoping that the two of you could watch Milo. Dad and I have to go somewhere," she explained.

"Where?"

"A friend of ours passed away, and we are going to the wake. Tomorrow's the funeral. So we'll be gone tomorrow too, but if you want, Matt can spend the night tonight and tomorrow. Provided you do your homework, of course."

"I have no opposition to this," he responded. But instantly, alarm wrenched through him. His stomach began to churn. What's going on, he wondered.

"I know it's a school night, but your father said Matt seemed lonely and was worried, and that's why we've agreed to let him spend the night. Also, he'd be helping us with Milo."

"I see." In spite of her reassurance, he couldn't shake the notion that there was more to this than meets the eye.

Matt had walked three blocks when Garrett's mom pulled up beside him.

"Hey, Matt," Garrett called from his open window.

"Hi. Uh, what's up?"

"Mom and I are giving you a ride. Also, you can stay at my house for the next two nights."

"What?" he asked as he got in the back.

"We would like you to stay with Garrett and Milo at the house tonight while we attend a friend's wake. Tomorrow afternoon is the funeral, and we hoped you'd both take care of Milo while we're gone. We figured you could just spend the night both nights," Mrs. Lee explained.

"Er, sure. I don't mind watching Milo. Thanks for offering to let me spend the night. It'll be great not having to walk so far to school."

"I'll stop by your house so you can grab some clothes and stuff."

"Okay."

Garrett poked him. "What happened to Bobby and Jeff?"

"Bobby had practice today, and Jeff went with Randy."

"Ah."

When they got to Matt's, he packed what he needed in his backpack. He couldn't believe he got everything to fit in with all his books and stuff. He checked all the doors and made certain they were locked then returned to the car.

"You got everything you need?" Garrett's mom asked.

"Yeah."

"All right, we're off."

As soon as they came through the door, Garrett's father approached them. "Hey, Matt. Glad you came. Milo will be happy you're here. He may play games with you, but don't let him get too worked up, okay?"

"Gotcha."

"Good. Garrett?"

"Yes?"

"There are some steaks in the fridge for your supper. We're going out to eat after the wake, so we'll probably be home late."

"All right."

"We're not leaving for an hour, so you guys can hang out until then," his mother added.

"Sweet," Garrett said.

Matt followed Garrett down the hall. "Gar, your room is the other way."

"Duh. But Milo must be in his room. I need to check on him."

Matt frowned. Garrett had never been an uncaring brother, but Matt had never seen him this attentive and sober. He held a fist under his chin, as if focused on many things. *I wonder if he feels it, too*, Matt thought. *Maybe he's worried for Milo's future as well.* They reached the door, and Garrett knocked. There was no answer. Matt entered behind him. Milo was sitting up in bed. His glossy stare was directed at his TV.

"Milo?"

He continued staring at the television screen for a moment before turning his head toward Garrett. "Garrett, why do you keep coming in here?"

"Just checking on you."

"Am I gonna die or something?"

Matt blanched. The color drained from Garrett's face. He trembled and said, "Don't be silly. Why would you think that?"

"Cuz you never come in here, and now it's like every day. I had a dream where you said you'd protect me. I don't know from what."

Garrett swooned. Alarmed, Matt said, "You okay, man?"

This got Milo's attention. "Bro, are you sick, too?"

"No, Milo. I'm fine. Just vertigo," he rasped. "Anyway," he added when he'd recovered his voice, "when did you have that dream?"

"Last night," Milo told him. He gazed at Garrett with open concern.

"I see. Well, if I am to protect you, dear boy, it's probably from cooties."

Milo made a face. "That's easy. All I have to do is stay away from girls."

"That could be a problem. You see, Liz is a girl, and I know you have a crush on her."

Milo flushed. "Do not."

"Then why're you blushing?"

"You're mean, Garrett."

"And you're a boy with a crush," he teased.

"Booger-face," retorted Milo, coughing a little.

"Did you hear that, Matthew? Them's fighting words."

"Knock it off, Gar."

"Thanks, Matt," Milo replied.

"No problem, bud."

"Matt, Mom and Dad said you're gonna spend the night. Will you play PlayStation with me?"

"Later. But you should rest up, 'cause me and Garrett are gonna play you at Sonic."

"That's my favorite game," he remarked.

"I bloody well know that, given that it's the only one you ever play," Garrett interjected.

"It's the only one I'm good at. I'm not as good as you," he said.

Garrett's eyes softened. He tousled Milo's hair. "Someday, I will teach you, young knight."

Milo laughed. "Promise?"

"Of course."

"Cool." An awestruck expression was on Milo's face.

Aw, he's so adorable, Garrett thought.

"Come on, Gar, let's go. We'll see you in a bit, Milo. I'll play you while Garrett cooks our dinner. How's that?"

"Yay."

When they were out in the hall, Garrett said, "Matt, I was going to—oh, never mind. You sure made him happy."

"What were you saying?"

"I was gonna have you help me with dinner. You know, cut things up and make the salad."

"Sorry."

"It's fine. You and Milo are free to have fun. But you are gonna help me with the dishes."

"Deal."

"So what shall we play before Mom and Dad leave?"

"Want to go old school and try to finish Spear of Destiny?"

Spear of Destiny was an old DOS computer game, the sequel to a game about fighting Nazis called Wolfenstein, that came out in the 1990s, a few years before they were born. But when Matt was a little kid, his dad had been big on the Wolfenstein franchise and all things by ID Software, Apogee, and other companies and had gotten him and Garrett hooked as well. Over the summer, Matt and Garrett had a bout of nostalgia and began playing Wolfenstein and Spear of Destiny again.

"Ah, Wolfenstein. Yes, let's."

They started the game using Dos Box and loaded their old save file, bjownsnazis. They had saved on level seven, switching off between levels. After about five levels and getting lost several times, Garrett grumbled, "You know, I'm starting to think that the gents at ID Software really hated the player."

Matt laughed. "I have to agree."

"What is with all the bloody mazes?"

"ID seems to've had a fascination with mazes," Matt observed.

"Yes, well, I don't," Garrett retorted.

When his parents left, Garrett and Matt moved into the living room. Milo wandered in to watch them battle on the PlayStation. A couple of hours later, Matt started Sonic with Milo while Garrett retreated into the kitchen. He took the steaks out of the refrigerator and placed them on a pan. Using seasoning salt, garlic salt, onion salt, a little bit of pepper, and a generous dose of Worcestershire sauce, he coated both sides of the steaks. Next, he dug out the broiler pan from the drawer below the oven, filled the bottom with a little bit of water, put the lid back on, and set the steaks on top. Once he got that in the oven, he set the timer for seven minutes. After that, he grabbed a plastic bag from the fridge, which contained part of a Vidalia onion.

He chopped half of the remaining onion and put the rest back in the fridge. Now for the lettuce, he thought. He took the head out of the crisper and got the huge salad bowl out of the pantry, along with the strainer. Then he set to work rinsing and prepping the lettuce. The timer went off, and he pulled the rack with the broiler pan out some, flipped the steaks, and shoved the rack back into the oven, resetting the timer. He'd probably have to leave one steak in for a minute or so longer, since Milo liked his well done.

From the cabinet above the microwave, he grabbed a bottle of Apple Cider Vinegar, a bottle of Wesson Oil, and a packet of Italian seasoning. These he carried to the sink. He grabbed the salad dressing bottle from the cabinet above the sink and dumped in the vinegar and oil, along with a little water and the Italian seasoning. He placed the lid on it and shook it. Awesome, he declared.

When all the steaks were done, he placed them on a meat platter and emptied the broiler pan into the sink. After finishing up the salad, he dished it out and set out plates, napkins, and silverware. He set Milo's steak on his special, little kid plate.

"Okay, children, dinner," he called.

"Ooh, it smells good. Did you make mine well done?" Milo asked.

"I did indeed," Garrett responded, setting the plate before him, along with a bowl of salad.

"Aw, man. You didn't make any potatoes," Matt observed, sounding bummed.

"You never asked me to make potatoes. Besides, you wanted to eat sooner rather than later, right?"

"Yeah, but your fried potatoes and French fries are so killer."

"Another time, Matthew. Now eat up. Besides, darest you ask me to make potatoes with the humidity so high today?"

"What's that got to do with anything?"

"It really shows that you never took Home Ec. It takes forever to get potatoes cooked right when it's humid outside."

"Really? Wow."

"Uh-huh."

Matt bowed his head before his plate, his hands folded up under his chin. Without speaking, he gave thanks for the food. Garrett smiled a little. He and his family were believers, he would say, but they weren't as formal when it came to dinner. Hm, why don't we ever say grace, he wondered. After the blessing, Matt ate heartily. The salad was great, though Matt didn't share their love of Italian dressing. He preferred French dressing. And he wasn't used to onion being in his salad. He thought it tasted quite fine, but he was used to his parents' way of making salad. All they ever put in a salad was tomato and, on occasion, bacon bits and croutons.

"I know you like tomato," Garrett said, "but I had none, or I would have added it to the salad."

"Oh, it's fine. Everything's delicious as usual."

"It's simple fare and simple preparation. You act like it's a five star meal. I didn't even make a three-course dinner."

"It tastes like one," Matt complimented. Milo seconded this.

"Geez, Matt, doesn't your mother ever cook?"

"She does when she's home. But lately she's been gone a lot."

"Ah. So, Milo, that good, eh?"

"Uh-huh," he mumbled, his mouth full.

"You could have swallowed first. I would have waited."

"You asked me when my mouth was full."

Garrett rolled his eyes. "Whatevs. Such is the logic of a six-year-old."

"Gar, will you play Sonic with me when we're done?"

"After we finish the dishes, dear chap."

"I can do them, if you want. That way you can play with him."

"You sure you don't mind, Matt?"

"Yeah."

"Hooray. Funsies."

When they were done eating, Garrett followed his brother into the living room. He snatched a controller and sat on the couch beside Milo. "You're on, little brother."

Milo coughed, then yelled, "Oh yeah? Bring it."

"Someone's gotten feisty all of a sudden."

"I'm gonna beat you!"

"Dial it back a little, Milo. Otherwise Matt and I will get in trouble for getting you too riled up."

Milo huffed. "Okay."

Matt heard them jeer back and forth between each other as he washed the dishes and smiled. When the dishes were dried and put away, he joined them. At nine o'clock, they sent Milo to bed, and Matt said, "What do you want to do now?"

"We better get our homework done. I totally forgot about it."

"Me too," he admitted, feeling guilty.

They went to Garrett's room and started on the horrid chore. A dead silence fell among them for twenty minutes, until Garrett muttered, "Ugh, Brandenburg, you are my mortal enemy. I shall avenge myself."

"Sh," Matt scolded.

"Revenge," he declared.

Matt suppressed a smile and returned to his work. He was finished in half an hour. It took Garrett another ten minutes to declare victory over the high school establishment. He slammed his books closed and crammed them into his backpack. Matt grabbed their bags and put them near the door. Garrett was rubbing his eyes.

"You're tired tonight, huh?"

Yawning, he said, "Yeah. Hope you don't snore tonight, Matt. I'd like to experience the dream world for a bit."

Matt smirked. "I'll try not to. Just don't step on me when you get up in the middle of the night to go to the bathroom."

"I shall endeavor not to."

Matt laughed. Garrett spread a blanket on the floor, then handed him a pillow and a blanket to cover up with.

"Thanks."

"You're welcome, good sir."

Covering himself up, Matt leaned back against the pillow, staring at the ceiling. Garrett lay on his side above him, eyes half-closed. He was facing Matt's direction. He saw Matt turn toward him.

"Gar?" he whispered.

"Yeah?" Garrett mumbled.

"I don't know how to say this, but last night, I was suddenly overcome with concern about Milo."

Garrett's eyes flew open. "You don't have a bad feeling about his health, do you?"

"No. I was worried about his future."

"I know," Garrett said with a sigh.

"What do you mean?"

"I feel uneasy about his future as well. I can't explain it."

"Me too. But then I started worrying about his whole generation and future generations."

"Wow. Heavy thinking, eh? Do you suppose it might have to do with Norm Morriston?"

Matt gasped. "I do. It was him I was thinking about when this concern started."

"Bloody Matt. You really should have told me that."

"I just forgot is all."

"Fine, fine. Can we change the subject? I'm really getting creeped out."

"Sure."

"On an even creepier note, does it strike you as odd that my parents have not yet returned, and it's already ten o'clock?"

"They said they'd be back late."

"True. But when my father has to work in the morning, late means eight-thirty, nine o'clock."

"It is a little odd, but I don't think it merits suspicion."

"You're probably right. I'm just jumpy."

The situation with his parents and the events of the last few days gnawed at his mind. The two of them going to a wake and tomorrow to a funeral was in itself a legitimate action, but he could not dismiss the idea that this was more than meets the eye.

Matt, oblivious to his anxiety, replied, "I guess maybe we both are."

Garrett did not respond. *I don't think Mom and Dad would lie to me about going to a friend's funeral, but I wonder if there's something else going on, too.* He rolled onto his back, his mind wandering. *Could they be visiting doctors in secret, maybe? What if Milo is seriously ill, and they don't want to let on?*

"Night, bud," Matt murmured.

Matt didn't expect a reply, assuming he was asleep. Garrett did not hear him. He gazed at the shadows surrounding them. Matt faded off before he did. Three minutes before midnight, Matt awakened with a jolt. He looked up at the clock on the dresser. 11:57 p.m. He could not remember the dream he'd been having, but sensed that it had not been unpleasant. Though he was confused as to why he awoke, his befuddlement was interrupted by an image of several black helicopters flying over a field in the fall. The cornstalks and grass were brown. *A war is coming, but it's not the people versus the government,* he thought. As soon as this thought was formed, his heart throbbed in his chest. Sucking in a deep breath, he figured it would take a while for him to get back to sleep, but he dropped off swiftly.

He was wrested from sleep not long afterward. He sat up. Again, he was certain that whatever he'd dreamt about was not bad. But, as he glanced at the clock, his focus sharpened even more. It was 12:57 a.m. In his head, he saw black choppers flying over a field, as if preparing to drop bombs. *A war is coming, but it's not the people and the government,* he thought. His head pounded, his chest tightened. Yet he was asleep less than five minutes later.

Matt jerked awake again. He had been having a good dream, though he could not remember it. He stared at the clock. It was 1:56, now 1:57. His eyes landed on the clock right as the numbers changed. The sight of a field with black helicopters overhead invaded his mind. A war is coming, but it's not the people and the government. Shivering, he wondered, What is with this war-is-coming business? No answers came to him. He leaned back against the pillow and turned his head toward the bed. Garrett was sleeping. Matt tried to relax, but couldn't.

A few seconds later, Garrett said, "Sneaking up behind me, eh? I think not."

Matt sprang up into a sitting position, his heart leaping into his throat. He breathed a sigh of relief when he realized Garrett was just talking in his sleep.

"No, I don't want these chickens. If I did, I would have bought them. Away with your un-purchased poultry."

Matt snickered. One of these days, I'll have my digital recorder with me and get this on tape, he thought. He lay back and was just nodding off when Garrett sat up. Matt saw him get out of bed, rub his chin, and head out the door. Sensing he was not on his way to the bathroom, Matt got up and tailed him. Garrett headed toward Milo's room. He stopped at Milo's door and entered without knocking. Matt crept up to the doorway. He pushed it open a little. Garrett stood beside the bed with his hand on Milo's forehead. His head was lowered, and his eyes were closed. He's praying, Matt realized. He closed his eyes and bowed his head, adding a prayer along with Garrett's. Upon opening his eyes, he saw Garrett caress his brother's face, staring at him.

"You better get healthy soon, Milo. I don't think my heart can stand worrying over you like this," he whispered. Then he kissed Milo's brow and started toward the door.

Matt backed away from the doorway. Garrett came out and shut the door. He turned around and uttered a gasp, beholding Matt with wide eyes and struggling to thwart a scream.

"Sorry, Gar," Matt whispered.

"Are you trying to drive me to my grave?" he muttered.

"No. I just came to see if you're all right."

"I'm bloody fine now. You've shocked my heart into submission."

Matt looked away. "Sorry."

"Well, now that you're here, come on," he said.

"What are we doing?"

"I want to see if my parents got home."

"I'm sure they did."

"Just humor me."

"Fine."

Garrett snuck to the end of the hall. When they arrived at his parents' room, he turned the door handle gently and pushed it open a few inches. From the doorway, they could see two shapes in the bed. Garrett closed the door, lost in thought.

"There, you see?" Matt said.

Garrett walked past him, ignoring his statement. Matt trailed him to the kitchen then outside to the garage. Garrett used the keys he'd snatched from the counter to open the side door, stepped inside, and flipped on the light. Both cars were in the garage. Without comment, he switched off the light, exited, and locked the door.

When they got back to his room, Matt asked him, "What was that all about?"

"I don't know. I'm just in a very cautious mood."

Wow, Matt thought, noticing his sober expression, he's worried about something. Garrett didn't even crack a joke about his odd actions. Matt cringed on the floor, uncomfortable with the silence and further alarmed when Garrett turned on the light. Gar grabbed a pen and fished a notebook out from between his mattresses.

"What is that? What are you doing?"

"It's a journal. I need to write this down."

Matt groaned. "Come on, man. I want to go to bed."

"Go ahead," he said, waving at Matt's spot on the floor.

"Why are you writing this down?"

"Humanity has a need to keep records. Besides, this helps me think and keep things straight."

"Are you sure that's all?"

"No, that is not all. Life is all. A game emulates it. A story tells it. Art imitates and illustrates it. Rulers try to control it. Overseers want to blind people to it. Evil mocks and tries to redefine it. Many societies have cursed it," he remarked.

"That's cryptic."

"No. Actually, it's quite simple and straightforward."

"Whatever you say."

Garrett wasn't listening. His inner world was rocked by a sudden declaration which he knew he should understand but did not. It's amnesia, he realized. The task is to discover who you are and what your mission is. Then you have to go about carrying it out. He wrote this down.

"Mattie, read this statement here, the last three lines. It just came to me, and I think you can use it for the game story."

He read it over and whistled. "Wow. Yeah, that'll work nicely."

"Shall we call it a night?"

"Yes."

Garrett shut the light off, and they finally fell asleep.

The Events of a Thursday

AT SIX A.M., Matt was awakened by a frightful noise. He shot out of bed and watched as Garrett's arm lazily landed atop the off button for the alarm clock. Because when he actually slept, he was a sound sleeper, Gar always kept the volume on the loudest setting. This had earned such ire from his parents that he now resided in this room on the other side of the house. He turned off the alarm, stretched, and looked at Matt.

"I'm gonna get a shower. You want to snooze while I'm doing that?"

"Yep."

"Okay, then. See ya in a bit."

Matt nodded and closed his eyes, enjoying the darkness. Instead of falling asleep, however, he found himself puzzling over Garrett's sudden attentiveness to Milo and his insistence that they make sure his parents had arrived home. Why's he so suspicious of their going to that wake, Matt wondered. Then again, how many parents let a friend sleep over for even one night during the school week, let alone two? Perhaps this was what had alarmed him, for they had never done this before. Matt's heart fluttered.

"Matt?" Garrett said from the doorway.

Matt took a deep breath and let it out slowly. "You done already, Gar?"

"Yes. I am sufficiently clean."

"My turn, then."

"You want me to make something for breakfast?"

"Do you have time?"

"If I make something easy."

"Sure."

"Awesome."

Garrett headed into the kitchen. I'm thinking French toast. Maybe I'll make extra for Milo, he decided. Humming, he busied himself. When he was done, he set a plate of French toast and a glass of orange juice on a serving tray and took it to Milo's room. He opened the door with one hand, balancing the tray in the other. He set the tray on the nightstand and shook Milo awake.

"What're ya doing?" Milo asked, yawning.

"Made you French toast."

"Thanks." He smiled.

"How ya feeling?"

"A little better."

"Good. Eat up, and then bring your dishes to the kitchen."

Milo scowled. "But I'm sick. You should come and get them."

"You're not an invalid, Milo."

"Ugh. Fine."

Garrett left him and plowed into Matt as he was coming down the hall.

"Sorry, bro."

"It's all right, Gar. At least you don't have cooties."

"That you know of," he added. "Liz may have already contaminated me."

"I think that would be the other way around. So what'd you make us?"

"French toast."

"Cool."

Once they had eaten and cleaned up, they grabbed their backpacks and headed out. As they walked, Matt suddenly remembered what it was that he'd wanted to ask Garrett the other night on the porch.

"Oh, hey. Did you ever figure out how to work XNA?"

"No, I have not. But Randy's gonna help me over Christmas break. Once he teaches me C Sharp, I shall teach you."

"Deal. So have you done any playthroughs lately?"

"I'm recording one with commentary right now."

"Cool."

"My last one has gotten several comments as of late about how my commentary ruins the video. Fortunately, most of the comments seem to be in my favor."

"That's because you're hilarious."

Garrett grinned. "If you say so."

"I do," Matt insisted.

When they reached the school, Garrett pointed and said, "Come, Matthew, let us enter this dungeon and face our doom."

"I'd rather face my doom than go to P.E."

"As would I. I'd almost rather have two classes with Brandenburg."

"Wow."

"I know."

They parted on the upper floor on the way to their lockers and met up again on their way to second period, which was Mr. Brandenburg's class. They shared third period too, which was P.E. Matt and Garrett chatted as they entered the locker room. Class was boring as usual: they played soccer. Matt didn't mind playing sports, but Gar found it dull. As they changed out of their uniforms after class, Matt saw two guys walking over to Garrett. *Uh-oh, Dustin and Joel. This can't be good,* he thought. Garrett had his back to the boys, but he heard their snickering. His heart raced. *Not again,* he pleaded in silence.

"Hey, look. It's the freak. You gonna go home and play World of Warcraft, loser?" Dustin Dodge mocked.

"Can he even hear us, or is he too busy living in his fantasy world?" Joel Richards asked, knocking his fist against the top of Garrett's head.

Dustin punched Garrett between the shoulder blades. "Come on, pansy, fight back."

Joel whacked him in the back of the neck, then grabbed him by the shirt collar and hoisted him off the bench.

"Knock it off. Just leave me alone," Garrett said.

"Look Dustin, the weirdo's gonna cry. What a baby."

They shoved him back and forth between themselves. "At least put up a fight," Dustin demanded. "I dare you, chicken-face. If you got the guts," he added.

Garrett stared at his locker with apparent fascination.

"Tell you what. I'll give you a free shot. I always give the ladies a freebie. Go ahead, hit me," Joel taunted.

Ignoring him, Garrett bent to grab his bag, face stoic. Matt walked over right as Dustin pushed Garrett, and he went flying head-first into the door of his locker, clocking the combination lock with brutal force. He blinked back tears. Matt forced his way in front of Garrett.

"Get out of the way, pee-wee," Joel snapped.

Although Matt was shorter than Garrett, he tried to shield him.

"Move it, Marshall, or I'll pound you, too," Dustin threatened.

Garrett straightened up and mumbled, "Just get out of their way, Matt."

Oblivious, Matt shoved Joel, who was closest to him. Joel fell over the bench. Dustin grabbed Matt by the throat and threw him aside. He landed a few feet from Joel. His heart pounded as he got to his knees. Garrett lunged forward, punching Dustin in the face. Dustin snarled, snatched Garrett by the hair, and slammed his head against the lockers. Garrett's ears rang. Joel scrambled to his feet and kicked Matt's legs out from under him, stomping on his back.

"You boys knock it off," shouted the locker room attendant.

The fight stopped. Smirking, Joel and Dustin slunk away. The attendant glared at Matt and Garrett.

"You troublemakers go to the office," he snapped.

"But they're the ones who started it," Garrett protested.

"You shouldn't have gotten them riled up. Go see the dean."

On their way out, Matt muttered, "I can't believe we're the ones who are getting sent to the office when those jerks started it."

"That's not called fascism, it's called fun," Garrett added, his voice dripping with bitterness.

"Are you all right?"

"Yeah. I think my skull is fine, though my brains are rattled, possibly scrambled like eggs. You?"

"I'm fine. My back hurts and my throat's a little sore, but otherwise good."

"Thanks for standing up for me."

"No problem."

When they got to the dean's office, she said, "I'm very disappointed to see you here."

"Mrs. MacArthur, it was Joel Richards and Dustin Dodge that started all this. They attacked me, and Matt stepped in," Garrett explained.

She graced them with a cool stare. "You two have Saturday school. You will remain here while I call your parents."

"Ma'am? My parents are on vacation," Matt told her.

"Then I shall send them a written notice of this occurrence, Mr. Marshall."

"What about Joel and Dustin?" Garrett questioned.

"They are not my concern right now."

"And yet you're punishing us? We're not troublemakers."

"Garrett Lee. That is quite enough of your mouth. If I had my way, I would suspend you both. Especially you, Mr. Lee. You're an empty-headed, lazy, worthless excuse of a student who will never amount to anything. Your kind add no value to society."

Garrett shut his mouth, eyeing her with hot disbelief.

Matt scowled at her. "You can't say that to him."

"Don't even get me started on you, Mr. Marshall. You have the presence of a gnat. You add nothing to this school: you eek by, leeching off certain productive students' popularity. You're an outcast, a waste. Both of you."

With that, she stormed out of the room to call Garrett's parents.

"Thanks for that, Matt."

"Dude, she is such an uppity, self-righteous crone."

"I prefer to think of her as Grade F Meat," Garrett whispered.

"I'll say. She's one bull of a lady."

"Don't call that thing a lady. She's nothing of the sort."

Silence fell between them. Five minutes later, Mrs. MacArthur came back and dismissed them with a curt nod. They met up with Jeff and Bobby in the cafeteria.

"Matt, what happened in Gym last hour? I heard you two got in a fight with some guys from the football team."

"Yeah, Bobby. Joel Richards and Dustin Dodge attacked Garrett."

"Matt jumped in to help," Garrett pointed out.

"We ended up getting Saturday school," Matt said.

"What? Why?" Jeff asked.

"Because Grade F Meat MacArthur saw it as our fault for existing," Garrett explained.

"That's absurd. You were defending yourself," Bobby said.

"That stupid MacArthur. I'd like to ream her out. So Dodge and Richards didn't get into any trouble?" Jeff said.

"No, Jeff," Matt told him.

"Man, that stinks," added Bobby. "If you want, I can teach them a lesson for you. I never liked them. Dodge and Richards are decent players, but they're useless off the field."

"Nah, better not."

"Well, if they bother you again, me and Jeff will rough them up, won't we?"

"Yeah," Jeff agreed.

"Thanks, guys," Matt said.

Garrett remained silent. Matt frowned. Poor Gar, he thought.

Bobby put a hand on Garrett's shoulder. "Come on, Gar. It's not that bad," he said.

Garrett responded with an awkward nod.

"Yeah, man. Those two are just jealous of your coolness," Jeff added.

Garrett's jaw dropped, but he remained speechless.

Matt gaped. Okay, Bobby's never called him Gar before, and am I going crazy, or did Jeff actually call him cool? "Dude, snap out of it," he interjected. "Brandenburg couldn't have fried your brain already."

Garrett managed a smile. "No, but give it another month."

Jeff laughed. "Brandenburg the bore, wish we had him no more," he sang.

"That is how everyone who encounters him feels, Jeffrey."

"There we go. There's the old Gar charm," Bobby remarked, punching him lightly on the arm.

"You don't by any chance have cooties, do you?"

"No, but Jeff might," he teased.

"I'm afraid I do not, good sir," Jeff said.

"Amazing. I give you props, Jeffrey, for your excellent mimicry," Garrett replied.

Jeff grinned. So this is what Matt sees in him. Am I bonkers, or do I actually like him now? I guess he is pretty entertaining.

"So, what's new with you two?" Matt asked.

"Jeff's sister went ballistic yesterday because he was in the basement working on something. Tell them, Jeff," Bobby said.

"Yeah, I was using the power saw, and she comes down whining because it's too loud, and she's trying to watch TV. I told her I had to finish this project for Shop class. She then told me that I should just be normal. So I shot back, 'Well, why don't you do something constructive?' And she a bottle of Pepsi bottle at me."

"Psh, Rachel and her temper," Matt remarked.

"It is fun to yank her chain, though."

"Remember the time she got sick of me talking and tried to shove a peach in my mouth?" Bobby asked.

"No."

"You were probably in the other room or something, man."

"Are you sure it wasn't one of the Bakers who did that?" Jeff joked.

"No. It was definitely Rachel."

"She is pretty memorable," Matt added.

Jeff narrowed his eyes. "You better not have a crush on her or anything, man."

"No. But with her temper, she's not easy to forget."

"Good. Although, she does think you're the least annoying of my friends."

"Really?"

"Yeah. But she still can't stand you."

"Not at all unexpected," Matt replied.

Garrett tapped him on the shoulder.

"Yeah?"

"I can stand you. Even when you snore."

"Thanks—I think."

"You're welcome."

Matt was surprised that neither Jeff nor Bobby made a joke about Garrett's statement. Aw, the two of them are growing up, he mused. The rest of the day went fine, but as he and Garrett left school, Matt saw a sad look on his face. Bobby and Jeff waved as they walked past.

"What's wrong, Gar?"

"I'm not looking forward to this, Matt."

"To what?"

"Going home. Mom's gonna be upset, and I don't even want to think about what Dad will say."

"It's not your fault, so they can't be mad at you."

"I'm not so sure they'll see it that way."

"What makes you think that?"

"It's just, last time the school called them after someone beat me up—like three weeks ago—they were pretty upset. Dad told me I should stand up for myself, and Mom cried."

"Did they yell at you?"

"Dad did, but it was one of those things where I knew he wasn't mad at me so much as angry at the situation, but I still didn't enjoy being yelled at."

"Right. I hear ya."

Garrett sighed. "Come on, we might as well get it over with."

"Okay."

Matt was puzzled. Three weeks ago, Garrett had said. But this had happened at least three times since then. *I guess he just never told anyone about the other times so nobody could call his parents,* Matt realized. He stared at Gar, shifted his eyes to the ground then glanced back up at him and back at the ground again. *I should have done more than just back him up, but what?*

"Stop it," Garrett insisted.

"Stop what?"

"Stop looking at me like that. You keep looking at me, then looking away. I'm not someone to pity," he said, choking up.

"Sorry."

"Stop feeling sorry for me. You've been defending me since kindergarten. You don't need to keep doing that. I can take it."

"But they shouldn't be bullying you."

"You're not my bloody protector, Matt."

"Why not? You're always there when I need you," he shot back.

"I have to be. I owe you. You're making my debt higher. Now how am I supposed to keep you from getting hurt if I keep dragging you into my battles?"

"You aren't dragging me into anything," Matt argued. "We're friends. And you don't owe me anything. We watch out for each other."

"I don't want to be the one to hold you back. Because you're friends with me, people put you down. By association, people consider you a loser. I'm dead weight to you."

He gasped. *I never knew he felt that way.* Tears slipped from Garrett's eyes as Matt glared at him. "Knock it off. I don't care what anyone thinks. I'm friends with you because you're cool. And if you make me get any mushier, I'm really gonna get mad."

Garrett's eyes widened. He wiped away the tears and struggled for a smile. "Very well, good sir. I shall attempt to man up."

"You'd better. A future owner of a gaming company doesn't become successful by berating his oddball genius."

Garrett roared with laughter. "I love how you felt the need to include the word oddball in that statement."

Matt grinned and shrugged. "The truth is the truth."

"Yes, Mattie. But you couldn't have said I was unique instead?"

"Oddball feels more accurate."

"Touche."

"On the plus side, did you notice that Bobby and Jeff seemed to have warmed up to you?"

"Of course. Well, I am their M.O.M. Although, I was concerned that Jeffrey might try to touch me like Bobby did. For then I would have needed a Hazmat suit, which I am sorely lacking."

"Ha. And when Bobby called you Gar, I about fainted."

"Indeed."

They traveled on in silence until they reached his house. "Oh look, here we are. How pleasant." As soon as they went in, he announced, "Mumsy, I'm home."

His mother came from the vicinity of the kitchen, hugged him, and began examining him. His father looked on from the doorway.

"Mother, what are you looking for?"

"Bruises. Because if I find even one, I'm gonna sue that school," she growled.

Garrett's face turned red. "They mainly got my head and neck."

She grabbed him by scruff of the neck, tilting his neck and head this way and that, her face close to his skin. Garrett looked past her and gave a tentative wave at his father, who did not wave back. His face was inscrutable. At last the inspection was concluded, and she peered into his eyes.

"Are you all right? It looks like you've been crying."

Though tears welled up once more in his eyes, he said, "I'm fine. How's Milo?"

"Don't try to distract me, young man." She went over to Matt and started inspecting him as well. He bore it with a sheepish expression.

"Mom, he's fine," Garrett told her.

"Really, I am, Mrs. Lee."

"Well, you're both lucky."

They nodded.

"That inept dean MacArthur called. She said that you've got Saturday school."

"Yeah."

"And what, may I ask, happened to the brutes who did this?"

"Nothing."

"That's it. I forbid you to attend Saturday school. That goes for you too, Matt."

"But we'll get into even more trouble," Garrett explained.

"Oh no, you won't. I am going down to that school tomorrow and giving that woman a piece of my mind. You just forget about it. I will handle it," she insisted with a wave of her hand and stalked off toward the bathroom.

Garrett cringed and looked at his father.

"Do as your mother says."

"Uh, okay."

"We'll be leaving in a few minutes. Milo's had lunch, but there's some ham in the fridge if you two are hungry. Also, your mother thawed out some chicken for you to cook for supper. We'll be home late again. Make sure Milo gets a bath and goes to bed at seven o'clock, because he's going to school tomorrow."

"Got it."

"Why don't you go get him and watch a movie or something?"

"Okay."

As they walked away, his father called, "Garrett."

He turned. "Yeah, Dad?"

His father stared at him, his expression still indecipherable. After a moment, he said, "Oh, never mind."

Garrett shrugged at Matt, and they went to get Milo. "That didn't go as bad as I figured it would," he said.

"I'm glad. So what movie do you want to watch?" Matt asked.

"I dunno. I'll let him decide." Entering Milo's room, he called, "Milo, want to watch a movie?"

"Yeah. What movie?"

"What do you wanna watch?"

"Ooh, can we watch *The Munsters* movie?"

Garrett chuckled. "Sure. I guess it's close enough to Halloween."

"Oh boy. Thanks, Gar."

Matt grinned. "Hey, remember when we used to watch that show late at night?"

"Ah, yes. Good ole Nick at Nite. Back when the programs they aired were good. I miss that."

Back in the living room, Milo and Garrett's mother came up to them and gave them each a hug. She kissed Milo's brow. "You guys be good. Milo, don't make a fuss about going to bed earlier than you have been. Listen to Garrett and Matt."

"Yes, Mom."

Their father arrived from the hall. "Have fun, kids. Matt, make sure Garrett does his homework."

"Right," Matt said.

When they left, Milo ran up to Garrett, brandishing a DVD in his hand.

"All right, Milo. Why don't you put that in the DVD player while I get us something to drink?"

Milo did as he said. "Can we have a snack with the movie?"

"You just had lunch."

He pouted. "But I'm still hungry, and I'm a growing boy."

Matt stifled a laugh, following Garrett to the kitchen.

"What are we having to drink?"

"I know you like tea, so we can have that. Picky little Milo gets lemonade."

"Sounds good to me."

After he made two glasses of tea and a glass of lemonade, Garrett went to the pantry.

"You hungry already?"

"No, but Milo is. Let's see. Ooh, I'll give him some graham crackers."

"Aw. You're a pushover, Gar."

"Perhaps."

He took the drinks for himself and Milo, as well as the graham crackers, and went back to the living room. Matt was behind him, sipping his tea. They sat next to Milo on the couch, one on either side.

"Here, I got you lemonade. You may also consume these graham crackers if you so desire."

"Thanks, Garrett."

"You're quite welcome."

At four-thirty, when the movie was over, Matt said, "You know, Gar, we really should get this homework done."

"Gah. You are way too neurotic. All right, we might as well. Then I'll make dinner."

"Deal."

"What am I supposed to do?" Milo asked.

"Isn't *Scooby Doo* on right now? You could watch that."

"Can I play Sonic instead?"

"Whatever. Here, I'll get it setup for you."

Garrett turned the PlayStation on and put in the game, then handed Milo the controller. "You know which button to press to start, right?"

Milo rolled his eyes. "Duh."

"Well, excuse me," Garrett shot back. "Bloody know-it-all Milo."

Milo hid a smile. Garrett met Matt in the kitchen, and they busied themselves with their studies. At six o'clock, Garrett started dinner. He turned to Matt.

"Do you want a salad tonight? Yay or nay?"

"Nay."

"Me either. I shall make some French fries. Fetch me the bag of potatoes from the pantry. On the floor to the left."

"Sure thing." Matt retrieved the potatoes and handed them to him.

"Thanks. Now while I peel and cut these, will you check on Milo? He's been way too quiet for the last half hour. I'm getting suspicious."

"Of course."

Matt went into the living room and saw the PS controller on the floor in front of the couch. Milo was nowhere in sight. The game was on the starter screen. Where'd he go, Matt wondered. He raced to Milo's room, but the door was open and the room empty. He checked their parents' room, to no avail. I wonder if he's in Garrett's room. As he trudged down the hall, a shadow zoomed past. Matt turned to see Milo running toward the living room. He went after him.

"Milo, where were you?"

"I had to go to the bathroom."

Man, I'm dumb. I should have checked there first, Matt thought. "Oh."

"Did you want something?"

"Gar asked me to check on you. You need more to drink?"

"Nah. And I'm done with the graham crackers."

"Okay. I'll put them back. Oh, so Garrett's making fries to go with the chicken."

Milo's face lit up. "Cool," he exclaimed.

"He does make good fries," Matt agreed.

"Only the best," Milo said. "Better than Mom's. But don't tell her."

"Ha-ha. I won't."

Matt returned to the kitchen to find Garrett marinating the chicken with lemon pepper dressing. His mouth began to water. "Man, that smells good already."

"I know. I'm tempted to eat it now, but alas, the possibility of illness and disease deters me."

"Milo is very excited about the fries."

"Did you tell him? Aw. I was gonna surprise him."

"Oh. Sorry."

"Well, at least he's happy about it."

"He said that your fries were the best, even better than your mom's, but that I shouldn't tell her."

Garrett beamed. "I shall not inform Mother of this, either, lest I should break her heart."

"She taught you everything you know, right?"

He nodded. "Almost. Some of my Home Ec teachers weren't complete buffoons, after all."

Dinner was done by seven-thirty. "Geez, I was supposed to have this done by now and have Milo in bed, but it looks like that's not gonna happen. Milo," Garrett shouted.

Milo came to the table. "What?"

"You have until 8:00 to finish eating and get to bed. Don't tell Mom and Dad that I let you stay up later than 7:00."

"Okay. But what about my bath?"

"Oh, crud. It's always something. We'll get you a quick one after you eat. And I mean quick."

"All right."

They ate in a hurry, and while Garrett helped Milo with his bath and got him ready for bed, Matt put the food away and took care of the dishes. It was 8:25 when Garrett came back. His hair was sopping wet.

"Phew. Milo is clean and in bed. I even read him a story. You finished the dishes and everything already?"

Matt nodded. "How'd your hair get so wet?"

"Milo decided to splash me."

"Yikes."

"We have some time before bed. You want to be a guest commentator on my recent commentary?"

"Sure, why not?"

"Hooray."

They spent the remaining time engaged in verbal tomfoolery. At ten o'clock, they called it a night, and by eleven, both were out cold. At 11:45, Garrett's parents arrived home and trudged to their room. When 2 a.m. came along, the house was still and quiet. In Milo's room, he snored softly. Deep into dreamland, he was unaware of the soldier standing at the foot of his bed. The soldier crossed his arms, his army coat riding up as he did so. His face was shadowed and serious, his eyes trained on Milo's sleeping form. At last, he turned and walked out. He would visit again when the time was right.

A few minutes later, Milo woke and sat up in bed. He glanced around, wary. He could swear someone had been there, standing by his bed. Yet there was no one around. *I don't think Gar was here*, he thought. He paused, straining his ears. Although he listened for several moments, he heard nothing. Throwing the covers aside, he got up and rubbed his eyes as he wandered down to the living room. Standing in the middle of the room, he glanced out the large picture window. Nothing outside held his interest. All at once, a vision burst into his mind. He saw a huge, wooden cross and a lion standing next to it, staring at him. Before he could react, a voice whispered, "Milo."

It was a quiet, tiny voice, but it scared him. He managed not to shriek as he bolted from the room. And he almost made it back to his room when he stopped dead in the hallway. He whirled around and crept down to the other wing, pausing outside Garrett's door. He stood there a moment, debating. At last, he pushed the door open. He could see Matt asleep on the floor, huddled under a blanket. His gaze traveled to Garrett's bed. His brother was tossing and turning, moaning. Milo's heart ached to see him so restless. Just then, his body quit moving. Milo's heart lurched. Garrett spoke, and Milo bit back a scream.

"Mr. Carlson, do you taunt me with those cookies? I think you do."

Milo strained to hold in a laugh. *He talks in his sleep. I wonder what he's dreaming about.*

"Zombie, say hello to Mr. Shotgun," Garrett mumbled with a southern accent.

Milo rolled his eyes. *Gar's dreaming about video games*, he realized. With that, he started to close the door. Frowning, he reopened the door and entered the room. He skirted around Matt to Garrett's bedside. Reaching out his hand, he wiped it across Garrett's forehead and kissed his cheek.

"Mom and Dad were talking about some mean kids pushing you around. Be careful, Gar. I need you to be safe. 'Cause, 'cause I love you, Booger-face." A tear fell on Garrett's cheek. Milo jolted and hurried from the room.

Stubborn Determination

At six o'clock, Garrett rolled out of bed and got ready. He shook Matt awake before heading for the kitchen. His mother was sitting at the table. He could hear something sizzling on the stove. The delicious smell identified the fare as country-fried steak with biscuits and gravy.

"Good morning, Garrett. Milo told me you made him French toast for breakfast yesterday. That was very sweet of you."

"I was making it for me and Matt anyway."

"Where is Matt by the way?"

"Taking a shower."

"Oh. Did you remember Milo's bath last night?"

"Nope. But Milo did, and he reminded me."

"Good. Sweetie?" she asked.

"Huh?"

"Are you doing all right?"

Frowning, he said, "Yeah. Why?"

She squinted at him and sighed. "No reason."

"Uh, okay."

"Would you get Milo up? Breakfast is almost done."

"Certainly," he replied. After waking Milo, he encountered Matt in the hall.

"Something sure smells good," Matt observed.

"Mother is making country-fried steak with biscuits and gravy."

"Ah, cool."

"Yes. I am quite fond of her cooking. She makes a great breakfast, in particular."

"I'm gonna eat way more than both of you," Milo interjected from behind them.

"Nah-uh," Garrett said.

"Yes-huh," Milo insisted. He stuck his tongue out and raced for the kitchen.

After breakfast, Garrett grabbed his backpack and waited by the front door. Matt came in, hopping on one leg as he tried to tie his shoe.

"You're unprepared this morning, Matthew," he noted.

"I know. I'm still groggy."

"That's just the food settling. That's what happens when you eat a nice, country breakfast."

"I don't think it's just that," Matt remarked as they went out the door.

Garrett frowned. His mind flashed back to the conversation he and Matt had last Sunday morning after the fake mutt went missing. He'd been about to ask a question, but they were interrupted by Mr. Welker. Now, he weighed the pros and cons of posing that question. *I can't believe I've forgotten for almost a week*, he thought.

"So, Mattie, I am in a quandary right now," he said.

"As to what?"

"As to whether or not to further vex you about this business with the fiends who are plotting against you."

Matt stopped. "What is it now?"

"Well, you remember how we were talking after the dog disappeared, and Mr. Welker came up?"

"Yeah?"

"I was about to pose an inquiry. Mr. Welker drove the thought right out of my head. But now I have remembered, and it is quite bothersome."

"Just tell me," Matt said with a moan.

"Very well. I was gonna say that someone had to have been inside the house Saturday night, because someone had to open the blinds. So when did someone get in?"

Matt's eyes widened. His throat closed up, and he bent over. Garrett grabbed him and yanked him back up. "Calm down. We'll figure it out."

He sucked in a deep breath and yelled, "What if someone's still there?"

"If it worries you that much, I'll come with you. We'll search the house top to bottom."

"No. I'll do it myself."

"You don't have to do it alone."

"Gar, you're a huge help, but I need to do this myself. Besides, I am miffed now. I pity whoever dares to trifle with me."

He sighed. "Fine. But I don't like leaving you at the mercy of an unknown threat."

"I've got to deal with it some time. Might as well be today."

"Just call me and let me know you're all right later, will you?"

"Deal." For a moment, Matt was quiet then he said, "I would like to know when the person came in."

"Maybe when we were out looking at the dog," Garrett suggested.

"No. I was in and out twice. There's no way someone would have had time to slip in the house then."

"I don't get it."

"What?"

"Hm? Oh, nothing. I was just thinking out loud."

Matt squinted at him. "You're hiding something. Tell me, Gar."

"I was wondering why I never heard anyone in the kitchen. I was awake during the time period in which someone had to have opened the blinds. Unless…"

"Unless what?"

"Well, I wasn't going to tell you this, but while I was trying to sleep, I heard that bloody wailing again. Maybe that covered the noise of the intruder."

"Or distracted you. Why were you afraid to tell me about that?"

"Well, you were so freaked. I didn't want to get you worked up."

"You gotta stop worrying so much. I can handle this. No more secrets."

"Fine. I will tell you all that pertains to you and this bizarre situation. You shall have the knowledge that many have craved yet not attained," he said.

Matt rolled his eyes. "Okay."

"Matt?"

"What?"

"You haven't kept anything from me, have you?"

Matt thought of the voice which told him that a fire of resistance burned in him. Best to just keep that one to myself, he thought. "No."

"Okay. I am pleased," Garrett responded.

"Great," he returned, his voice low and serious.

He frowned and glared out at the road ahead of them. Reckless anger coursed through him. Furrowing his brow, he stepped forward with purpose. Garrett's eyes widened as he watched this transformation. Wow, he's like a warrior about to battle a vicious foe. A smile played about his lips. I always knew you had a hero's guts in you, Matt.

They parted company on the second floor of the high school, and Garrett entered first period with a thoughtful expression on his face. I hope you'll be okay, buddy, he thought, frowning. This concern came in addition to his worry about Milo. He groaned.

Meanwhile, Matt sat in his German class, staring a hole through the blackboard. These jerks are not gonna keep pushing me around, he decided. He was unable to concentrate on school at all until History. Upon realizing this, he covered his mouth with his hand, lest he burst out laughing and irk Mr. Brandenburg. Garrett poked him from behind.

"Psst, what's up, Matt?"

"I'll explain later," he whispered.

"Mr. Lee, Mr. Marshall, do you have something constructive you wish to add to the lecture?"

"No, sir," they replied.

"Then might I suggest that you shut your traps and listen?"

"You certainly may," Garrett returned.

"Mr. Lee, zip your lips. I've had about all I can stand from you this week. You are to be silent the rest of the class, or you and I shall become quite intimate during your after school time. Do I make myself clear?"

Garrett nodded. The rest of the class snickered.

"Quiet down and stop acting like a bunch of first graders," Mr. Brandenburg scolded.

The next period was P.E. Garrett trembled on the way into the locker room. Matt held his breath. Garrett's muscles tensed up as he changed into his uniform. So far, so good. No one bothered him. He and Matt exited the locker room with a relieved sigh. Class ended up being pretty easy. The entire duration was spent in the weight room lifting weights. He and Matt weren't super strong, but at least this was an activity they could do without interacting with the rest of the guys. When it was time for them to go back and change again, Garrett cringed. As he opened his locker, he hunched his shoulders without realizing it. This time, no one came near him. At last, fully dressed once more, he looked around. Only Matt was nearby.

"You ready, dude?" Matt asked.

"Yeah."

They hurried to the cafeteria and grabbed a seat.

"What was going on in Brandenburg's class? Were you all right?" Garrett asked.

"Yeah," he assured. "I had to stop myself from laughing because I realized that I was unable to concentrate on anything academic until he started speaking."

Garrett cracked up. "Hilarious. And it's all irony, too."

"Ironic," Matt corrected. "So, was your concern worth Brandenburg's ire?"

"Oh yeah. Did you hear him tell me we'd become quite intimate if I didn't stop? Ew."

"I know. I can't believe you had the gall to be like, 'You certainly may.'"

Grinning, he said, "Someone has to challenge him. Teachers need that, y'know. Good for their health."

"Right," Matt said, rolling his eyes.

"So, are you sure you want to explore your house for danger alone?"

"Yes," he replied, gritting his teeth.

"Okay." Garrett sighed.

"Let me do this on my own."

"But you always help me out whenever—"

"I know, but Gar, I've relied on you way too much already. And you know if it gets too serious, I'll call you for reinforcement."

"Oh yeah, the enforcer. I like the sound of that. I'll enforce you all the way to oblivion. Okay, no. But Matt?"

"Yeah?"

"You'd better call me if there's an iota of danger."

"Okay, okay," Matt assured him, a guilty smile on his face.

"You'd better. I'm not fooling. See the serious face? I've got my serious pants on," he lectured with a sober expression.

"I know."

"All right, then. Shall we go up and see what they've got to eat around here?"

"I suppose."

"Ah, cafeteria food. I'm slightly frightened, Matthew."

"Understandable."

"You guys got that right," came a voice. It was Bobby.

"Where's our friend Jeffrey?" Garrett asked.

"He and Randy are in the computer lab fiddling with Autocad."

"Ah."

"So, no one messed with you guys last hour, did they?" Bobby pried.

"Uh no," Matt mumbled, looking down at his tray.

"Good." Bobby smacked his fist against his palm. "I gave those two a personal lecture about bullying."

"Did you hurt them?" Matt inquired.

"Nah. I told them I would if they ever touched you again. So let me know if it happens again."

"Okay, Sir Bobby," Garrett answered.

Matt gawked as Bobby smirked. Wow, they're really getting along well, he observed.

When they got back to the table, Garrett said, "Matt, are you gonna skip Saturday school tomorrow? I'll have no choice, because of Mom."

"I dunno. I may go, but I don't want to upset your mom if she really came down here and chewed out MacArthur."

"Oh, she did," added Bobby, munching on a fry.

"How do you know?"

"Because Jeff saw her storming out of the office earlier."

"But he's never met my mom, so how'd he know it was her?"

"Two things gave it away. One was her calling MacArthur a pompous, incompetent, tyrant of a dean, and the other was Liz walking by and greeting her."

At Liz's name, Gar's eyes softened. "What'd Mom say to her?"

"She said hello and something about her mother. That's all I remember from what Jeff told me."

"Aw."

"Where is Liz, anyway?" Matt asked.

"If you must know, she's been going home during lunch a few times a week to check on her mom."

"What's wrong with her mom?"

"She just had surgery, and she's getting around pretty good and all, but Liz worries about her when she takes her medicine. She gets really dizzy, and Liz is afraid she'll fall or something. Randy would do it, but he has to stay for lunch, because he usually works after school."

"Oh wow. So that's why she's hardly around lately."

"Yep. There are times I barely see her, but we talk on the phone or on Facebook a lot."

"You should have told me, man. I would have sent her mom a card or something."

"Sorry, Mattie. I didn't think to tell you."

"I'll add her mom to my prayer list."

"Thanks. I'm sure Liz'll appreciate that."

As they walked out of school, Garrett threw his arms up and said, "Freedom! For another weekend, anyway."

Matt laughed as Garrett's mom pulled up and called to them.

"Hi, Mom. What brings you here?"

"I'm here to deliver some good news."

"Hi, Mrs. Lee," Matt greeted.

"Hello, Matt. I'm pleased to inform you both that I haven't received any calls from Milo's school today, so I'm sure he's on the mend. Oh, and you two no longer have Saturday school."

"Sweet," Garrett replied.

"Great," Matt said.

"Matt? Are you sure you don't want to stay another night?" she asked.

"I really should get home and clean the house," Matt lied.

"Well, here then. You forgot your clothes. I had a feeling you'd forget, since you were distracted this morning, so," she began, handing him a plastic bag, "there's your laundry, nice and clean."

"Thanks." Matt blushed. It was weird having someone else do his laundry for him. He'd been washing his own clothes since he was eleven. He glanced over to see Garrett holding a hand over his mouth, trying not to laugh at him.

"You're welcome. So, Garrett, how'd your day go?"

"It was quite a fine day, except for my smart mouth coming in contact with Mr. Brandenburg's lecture."

"How many times have I told you not to vex that poor man so?"

"Rather a lot. I know that."

"Stop agitating him. I mean it."

"Okay, I got it."

"Well, I've got to pick up Milo, so do you want a ride or do you want to walk home?"

"I believe I'm in a walking mood, Mother dear."

She smiled. "All right, see you when we get back. Before I forget, do you want something from Ottercreek Market? Milo and I are gonna stop at their cafe for lunch. We can bring you back something, unless you want to tagalong."

"Nah. You guys go ahead. But I would like you to bring me back something. Lunch was pretty awful today. Let's see. Um, a turkey club would be nice."

"Okay. See you in about an hour."

"Bye, Mom." He waved and turned to Matt, who was stuffing the plastic bag with his laundry into his backpack. "Bye, dear friend."

"Bye," Matt said as Jeff walked up. Garrett walked away with an exaggerated wave.

"Hey, man," Jeff greeted.

"Hi," Matt said.

Jeff was followed by Bobby. "C'mon, let's get outta here, guys."

"Sure," Matt replied.

He was relieved that he didn't have to walk all the way home alone. Only for a few blocks would he be by himself. As they walked and talked, a couple of junior high kids waltzed past them, laughing and shoving each other.

Matt tossed his backpack aside and locked the front door. He was gonna make sure this house was secure if it killed him. He searched all the rooms downstairs first. From the kitchen, he snatched the long carving knife and tromped down to the basement. The back door was still locked, the deadbolt engaged as he'd left it. After a cursory glance out at the yard, he rushed down the steps. It took mere moments to clear the entire basement. Scowling, he ran back to the kitchen and then upstairs. The front room was hiding no one. The guest room and the rec room were unoccupied. He went through his parents' room next.

Nothing there, either. He opened the closet, scouring it as he had all the other closets. No trace of anyone. Everything appeared undisturbed. He checked the door to the old deck. It was locked up tight. He even went through the bathroom and peered in the shower, as he had when making his circuit of the downstairs. Zilch. All that remained were his room and the attic. He sorted through the few items under his bed, moving them out of the way to make sure no one was hiding there. Then he poked around in the closet and found nothing concealed within. Last but not least, he thought as he climbed the attic steps. In one hand, he held the carving knife. In the other, he had his trusty baseball bat.

He moved about the large space, ducking behind and between boxes and other junk. There were no signs that anyone other than he had been up here in months, except for the bats. He spotted guano on several of the boxes and on the floor. Great, now he'd have to clean that up before he dragged the Christmas decorations down next month. Sighing, he figured it was now time to search the backyard.

Since the front yard was all open, he knew there was nothing of note there. His house didn't have a side yard on the right side, because of the driveway. However, he could see between his house and both of his neighbors' houses from the front yard and had ascertained that no threat was on either side. As Matt descended the attic stairs, a thought occurred to him. He stared out each of his bedroom windows, which looked out on the backyard. From up here, there didn't appear to be any intruders lurking around.

He paused and made sure all his windows were locked, then went through the entire upstairs again and checked every single window. All were secure. When he got downstairs, he hurried to each window and tested the locks. Everything was locked and sturdy. He hurried out back and traced the lawn. With the snow melted, the lawn was muddy. *I should have put some plastic bags* on my shoes, he realized as his feet sank into the ground. He found no traces of an intruder.

He removed his shoes outside the back door before entering the house. After sliding the carving knife into the knife block and cleaning off his shoes, he picked up his backpack and fished out his laundry. Opening the plastic bag, he extracted the clean clothes and set them on the dining room table. With a bored sigh, he went to the refrigerator. Today, he'd managed to get all his homework done before he left school. His teachers had been generous, giving very few assignments.

Matt grabbed the plastic Tupperware of leftover stroganoff. He lifted the container and paused. Setting the container aside on the kitchen table, he rummaged through the fridge. What the heck? I could have sworn I had two containers of this stuff leftover. He hadn't eaten any since the night he'd made it, so where'd the other container go? It wasn't in the fridge. Frowning, he went over to the sink. There were no dishes in the sink, which was as he'd left it. He opened the dishwasher and bent over, peering inside. Nothing inside. I wonder, he thought. He trekked over to the pie safe, where the Tupperware and storage containers were kept.

As he sorted through the safe's contents, he spotted the very one he had used to store the rest of the Hamburger Helper. He snatched the plastic dish, examining it. It was clean. Picking up the lid, he was just about to put it back on, when he noticed a very faint spot in the corner.

Matt scratched it off with his fingernail. It was the same color as the sauce from the stroganoff. His eyes narrowed, his heart beat grew frantic. He slammed the lid on the container and threw it back inside the pie safe. I'll eat and then call Gar, since the house is secure, he decided.

Garrett arrived home, grateful that no one had tailed him. He walked into his room, inhaling the quiet. Not too much homework today, so I shall do it now and get it over with. Boy, Matt really has had an influence on me, he mused as he set to work. An hour later, as he was wondering what had become of his mother and brother, as well as his turkey club, his cell phone rang. He glanced at the screen. Oh, it's Matt. He picked up the phone.

"Greetings, Matthew."

"Gar, I'm calling to let you know how things went."

"Oh, right." He'd forgotten about that. I shall place the blame for this on Mr. Brandenburg, he decided, because he threw me off by not giving us much homework.

"The house is unoccupied, but I did notice one odd thing."

Garrett straightened up in his chair. "What's that?"

"Well, either someone was here at some point and left, or one of the ghosts has a thing for Hamburger Helper stroganoff."

Garrett uttered a noise that was half-shout, half-laugh. "Okay, explanation needed."

"I had two containers of stroganoff left Tuesday. When I came home, only one was in the fridge. So I wondered where the other container went. I searched the sink and the dishwasher. Not there. I looked in the pie safe, and there was the container, looking clean. Only, the lid had a tiny spot of sauce on it. It was barely noticeable."

"That is just…no. I'm sorry, no. That's all I can come up with right now."

"I know. Anyway, everything's all right."

"I appreciate the call. Is there anything I can do?"

"Nah. I'm fine. At least the house is secure now. I even checked the windows."

"Wow. Yep, can't be too careful when being stalked by wackos. Neuroticism pays off at last." He heard Matt laugh.

"You're right, dude."

"Aren't I always?"

"Not according to Brandenburg."

"Oh fie on him, good sir."

"He really didn't like your answer to his daily quiz question yesterday."

"Then he shouldn't have asked it."

"Come on, who expects an answer like that?" He deepened his voice a bit and mimicked their History teacher, "Mr. Lee, 'He was bloody hilarious in *Bill and Ted's Excellent Adventure*' is not an acceptable answer as to the historical significance of Napoleon Bonaparte. Especially as regards the Napoleonic Wars."

"Psh, he was just like that teacher in the movie. An overly serious stuff-shirt."

Matt snickered. "You're lucky your smart mouth didn't get you detention."

"Indeed I am."

Matt responded with a deep sigh.

"What's wrong?"

"Nothing. I'm just bored."

"Me too. I'm thinking of working on my commentary."

"Put it on Youtube when you're done so I can see."

"But of course. I always display my genius before the entire world. So's they can all learn from my example. Meh."

"I'll leave you to your commentary and talk to you tomorrow."

"Dandy."

"Bye."

"Buh-bye."

Matt hung up the phone and fetched his keyboard, stand, and his manuscript books. His hands wandered over the keys at random. He wasn't the most talented keyboardist, but he enjoyed it, and he wasn't bad by any means. When he had something interesting, he wrote down the notes and chord combinations in the pad he was using for the game theme. He even added accompaniment to the melody. The composition was about complete as he whiled away the time, exploring the keys. *This can either be the main theme, or it can be the hero's theme,* he decided.

When that was complete, he put everything away and checked the clock. It was past five. Time for some action. He took the PlayStation from his room, grabbed a few games, and set up in the family room. He was hoping against hope that he would get a PlayStation 4 for Christmas. He'd been hinting at his desire for one since March. But for now, he had to make do with the PS 3. He selected Silent Hill 2 to start with.

Garrett's body jerked. He was up and out of bed before he was even awake. He couldn't figure out why he was no longer asleep, but his eyes flicked toward the clock. 3:14 a.m.? *I can never just stay asleep anymore.* He moaned. Something moved outside his bedroom window. He rushed over and peered outside, pulse racing. Pain welled up in his chest as he surveyed what was before him. There in front of him stood the soldier from Richard Street, beckoning.

Eyes widening, Garrett threw open the window. "Get out of here, before I call the cops," he threatened.

"Matt's in danger. You have to go to him."

"What? How do you know that? Who are you?"

"Better hurry. And do not take Richard Street."

Climbing out the window, Garrett said, "But if I need to hurry, that's the fastest way."

The soldier shook his head. "Avoid Richard Street from now on."

"Why?"

"You need to go."

Garrett glanced back at the safety of his room. He sighed. "I should probably grab a weapon."

"Take this. It's all you'll need." The man handed him a small, flat stone.

"How is this going to—you know what? I'm not even gonna ask. I'm just gonna go with it."

The soldier stepped back, smiling.

"You still haven't told me who you are."

"Later," he said.

"What do you mean later?"

The guy waved him off, fading away before his eyes. I did not just see that, Garrett thought. I'm gonna run. He sprinted away, grasping the stone in his palm. Sweat broke out on his forehead as he flew down the road. He didn't even consider taking Richard Street. When he reached the highway, he cut across without bothering to wait for the stoplight. Fifteen minutes later, he gasped for breath, standing at the end of Matt's sidewalk. The upstairs was dark, but he could see a light on in the family room through one of the front windows. Panting, he went up to the porch and rang the doorbell. No one came. He banged on the door, and still no one came. If Matt was downstairs, he was sure to be leery of whoever was at the door. Rats, I should've brought my cell phone. Panic tried to strangle him, but he shrugged it off. Now what?

Raising his fist again to knock, he paused and opened his palm. He was supposed to use this stone somehow. He left the porch and went to the driveway, approaching the side of the house. There was a side window in the library, which was in front of the windowless family room. Perhaps if he threw the stone at this window, he could get Matt's attention. He cocked his arm back, flung it forward, and turned on his heel and launched the rock at Mr. Welker's dining room window instead. He gaped as the stone smacked the glass with a loud thud. What just happened? Why did I do that? He heard Buster start to bark. Oh no, I'd better hide, he thought, racing around to the front of the house and ducking on the opposite side.

He took shallow breaths, still trying to puzzle out what had happened. Movement inside the living room window drew his attention. Matt was approaching the front door. Garrett leaned around the corner as Matt came onto the porch, glancing around with wide eyes.

"Psst, Matt, over here."

Matt recoiled and hurried over. "Gar? What're you doing here so late?"

"Let me in, and I shall explain."

Once inside, he rushed to the back landing. Matt tailed him, rubbing his eyes. Garrett turned on the floodlight, peering at the yard for several moments. Then he went outside. As Matt stood agape behind him, he slogged around the entire perimeter of the yard. When he was satisfied, he returned to the back door. His eyes, however, wandered to the back of the yard again, past the fence. Hm, I wonder, he thought.

"Gar, what are you doing? You're freaking me out."

"In a moment, Matt. I'm thinking."

"Can we at least go back inside?"

"Yes."

Mr. Welker stepped onto his back porch at that exact moment. He called to them. "Did you boys happen to see anyone throw something at my window? I heard a noise, and Buster started barking his head off."

"No. We came out to see what the noise was, too," Garrett lied. Matt eyed him with suspicion but played along.

Mr. Welker frowned and went to investigate the window that had been hit. He bent down, grabbed something, and came back over. "Looks like someone threw a rock at my window. Darn kids," he sighed. "I'll bet it was an early Halloween prank."

As soon as he mentioned Halloween, the hair stood up on the back of Garrett's neck. Buster came up to the screen door, growling. Garrett swallowed hard.

"Oh, Buster, shut up. It was just some fool kids up to no good." He opened the screen door and entered the house, bidding them goodnight as he shut the door.

Garrett pushed Matt along until they were inside again.

"Okay, what are you doing here?"

"First, I should mention that I'm the one who threw that stone at Mr. Welker's window."

"You jerk. Why'd you do that?"

"I don't know."

"What do you mean you don't know?" Matt said, raising his voice.

"Sh. What I mean is I was trying to throw it at your window."

"What?" Matt scowled at him. "You'd better have a good explanation for this."

"I was trying to get your attention. You didn't answer when I rang the doorbell or when I knocked. I figured you were freaked. I didn't have my phone to call you, so…"

"Wait. That was you at the door? I was creeped out. Sorry. But why'd you throw the rock at Mr. Welker's window instead?"

"That's the thing. My body just moved of its own accord. I couldn't help it. One second I was facing your window, leaning forward about to hurl the stone, then I just pivoted toward his window without even knowing I was going to. Then the stone left my hand."

Matt rolled his eyes.

"Oh come on. With all the things that have happened to you that I take your word for, and you don't believe me about this? You bloody well should," he snapped.

Matt frowned. "You're right. I'm sorry."

"Okay, then."

"What made you come over here at this time of night?"

"I snuck out because someone told me that you were in trouble."

"You snuck out? You never sneak out. Wait, who told you I was in trouble?"

"You'll never believe me."

"Try me."

"That soldier I saw a few days ago. I had a dream with him in it the other night. I was fighting a fire out in the backyard, and there he was."

"A fire?" Matt's eyes grew large.

"Yeah. Anyway, I woke up a little after 3 a.m., and here's that same soldier standing outside my window."

Matt gasped.

"So I opened the window and told him to get lost, or I'd call the cops, right?"

"Right."

"And he said you were in trouble, and I needed to go to you. He also told me not to take Richard Street ever again. Anyway, I was gonna grab a weapon, but he handed me the stone and said it was all I needed. So I came here, tried to get your attention by ringing the doorbell and knocking, decided to throw this stone at your window when that didn't work, and wound up getting Mr. Welker's window instead."

"Too weird."

"I know," Garrett panted.

"You wanna crash here?"

"Duh. I'm not walking back home."

"Won't your parents get mad?"

"I'll come up with something."

"Okay, I guess."

"Do you have anything to drink?"

"There's some cherry Kool-Aid in the fridge."

"That'll do."

"Hang on, let me get you a glass."

"That'd be exquisite."

When Garrett was refreshed, Matt retrieved his keyboard.

"Whatcha doing?"

"You have to hear this. I came up with some theme music for our game."

"Okay."

Matt played him what he had finished.

Garrett clapped. "That's fantastic. It's got the perfect mood to it."

"Glad you like it."

"See? And you always say you're not a good musician."

"Well, I'm not."

"Right. That's like saying I'm not good at video games."

"I can't believe you ran all the way here to save me," Matt said, changing the subject.

"Oh, yes. I almost forgot. I think the soldier must be a ghost."

"Why do you say that?"

"Because he disappeared right in front of me."

"Whoa."

"Yeah. That was pretty spooky."

"You seem to have survived the shock," Matt noted.

Gar nodded. "Because I have a will of steel. Fortified with vitamin B."

Matt cracked up.

"Glad to see you still find me funny."

"You'll always be funny."

"Even when I'm old and gray?"

"Uh-huh. Even if your jokes get steadily worse, you'll always be funny-looking."

"Gee, thanks, bro."

"You're welcome."

"Bloody Matt. You're always stealing my lines."

"Get over yourself."

"Oh, is that how it is? I make the journey here, running all the way, and all you do is mock me? You're a horrible person," he muttered. "Just an absolute, horridly rude, tremendously mean person."

Ignoring this remark, Matt said, "So what do you want to do now?"

"I'd like to sleep, but I know that's not gonna happen. So, I guess we could, er, converse with one another."

"How about we just try to get some sleep?"

"In this bloody house? I think not, sir."

"I've played video games for at least six hours straight, plus a couple hours earlier in the evening. I can play no more. But you are welcome to."

"Insomnia, Matthew?"

"Dude, it is a Friday night."

"Technically, it's a Saturday morning."

"Anyway, you play, and I'll watch from the couch."

"You mean you'll snooze. Fine, whatevs."

By five a.m., Matt was out like a light. The moment he noticed this, Garrett turned off the PlayStation and flipped off the light.

He stood in the doorway between the family room and the dining room for a moment, watching as Matt smiled in his sleep. For a while, he observed in silence, frowning. At last, he let out a sigh. An urgent pulse went through him, making his heartbeat race. Milo's face flashed through his mind.

Milo…Matt. The certainty that he should do something for them nagged at him. Grabbing a blanket from under Matt's feet, Garrett unfolded it and spread it over him. The urge to laugh came over him. *This mothering and fussing over everything is getting a tad bothersome,* he thought. *I feel bad if this is what parents go through. The nurturing instinct is excruciating, agonizing, and yet worth it. Hm, fancy that.* Perhaps he wasn't as regretful of the experience as he'd led himself to believe.

He looked down at Matt. "I got this one, bud," he said.

With that, he went into the kitchen and opened the basement door. Plodding down the steps, he thought about the fence at the end of the yard. Earlier, it had come to him that perhaps someone had been down at the abandoned brickyard. *That soldier told me that a stone was all I needed.* He recalled throwing it at Mr. Welker's window. *It's possible that I was meant to chuck that sucker at Welker's window all along. If that is the case, then the purpose must have been to alert Buster and get him barking,* he thought. So then, the way he'd warded off the threat to Matt was to cause a commotion and scare off the would-be intruder.

He grimaced as he unlocked the deadbolt. *Until his parents get home, Matt's very vulnerable. I'll do what I can.* Therefore, he resolved to have a look around the brickyard. Gar turned the floodlight on and paused. He didn't want to leave the door unlocked while he left Matt alone. He ran back to the kitchen and grabbed Matt's key chain, stopping to scribble a quick note, which he placed in Matt's hand. *Just in case he wakes up,* Garrett thought. He snatched a flashlight off the top of the fridge and took off.

Once outside, he locked the door and left through the fence gate. He had to trespass on Mr. Welker's property, but it was for a good cause. He trudged along until he got to the other neighbor's yard. He was unable to go straight down the hill behind Matt's yard, because the trees were too dense. So he walked down the neighbor's neat little path, keeping his balance by hanging onto the neighbor's fence when necessary.

Why didn't I take the entrance in the alley near the end of the street, he wondered as he climbed down the hill. As he reached the road at the bottom, it dawned on him that he had no weapon. He groaned. Too bad. I'm not climbing that bloody hill again to get one.

Sacrifice

Now, he could either follow along the road behind Matt's house or take the road that split from this one, paralleling the highway. Either way, he had decided to traverse the outer perimeter first and search the buildings afterward. I'll go down this one first, he decided, taking the latter road. Garrett crept along, sweeping the flashlight along the ground, scanning for signs that anyone had been there. Every now and then, he glanced up to gauge his surroundings. So far, there were no tire tracks or shoeprints, and nothing in the debris suggested intruders of the nefarious stalking sort.

His shoes crunched along the gravel. He tried walking slower, hoping to make less noise, but it was no use. Loose pebbles bounced off his feet as he walked. Although he was positive that whoever threatened Matt was long gone, that didn't mean the buildings were unoccupied. The numerous shadowy places for an enemy to hide frayed his nerves. Tall palettes of bricks formed rows and tight corridors at random intervals, adding a sense of chaos and confusion. He kept his eyes on the palettes as he edged farther down the road. A twig snapped beneath him as he crossed the bridge over the creek. Garrett clamped his mouth shut, biting back a shriek.

At the southeast corner of the lot, he made a right and walked to the southwest corner, where he turned and cut through the grass until he reached the northwest edge of the property. He combed through the tall grass with the flashlight as he headed back toward the road that ran behind Matt's. He paused just before the asphalt. Perhaps I'd better search the four buildings before checking out the hill, he thought. That way, he could be sure no one was observing him. If anyone was, his presence was doubtless known, but it was unavoidable.

Starting with the nearest one, he snuck in through a large hole in the door. Inside, it was bare. The place had been cleaned out. Although no furnishings or equipment remained, broken pieces of lumber littered the floor. Sawdust and brick dust coated the cement beneath the pieces of wood. To his right was a steel staircase that led up to four offices which were accessed via a small landing. Seeing nothing of note at present on the lower level, Gar climbed the stairs. Entering the nearest office, he perused the room with the flashlight. The office was essentially a ten by ten space which contained a battered desk and little else. Huh, so no one bothered to take this desk, but the chair was apparently good enough to cart off, he mused. Squatting on the other side of the desk, he opened the large top drawer. There was a dirty sticky note inside with handwriting on it. He shined the light on it. The faded writing was illegible.

He slammed the door shut and opened the top of three side drawers. It contained a package of rotting breath mints and two red ballpoint pens. Garrett narrowed his eyes and opened the next drawer. All it sheltered was a lonesome paperclip. Opening the final drawer, his eyes lit up. He snickered. What an odd combination. The drawer held three staplers, no staples, and a pint of Jack Daniels, half-empty. He left this office and entered the next one. There was a chair but no desk and a tall, metal shelf. He surveyed the shelves. A lone matchbook, a few blank pieces of paper, and a dry-erase marker were the only items remaining. Bloody fascinating, he thought with a scowl. The last two offices yielded nothing. There was no furniture of any kind inside, or anything else, for that matter.

Garrett tromped downstairs and made a few rounds over the ruined lumber and through the dust. Still nothing. He slipped out and walked to the next building. He was able to open the door, because it was unlocked. This building had a tall ceiling, just like the other one, but no upper floor. Machinery was still housed inside. He dodged all the dangerous looking stuff, having no clue what the machines were called or what they did. Other than the obvious question of why these machines were still here, which led him to wonder why there were stacks of bricks remaining outside, there was nothing of note. This is getting tedious, he grumbled, certain now that no one lurked in the brickyard.

He proceeded around the palettes of bricks to the third building. Surprise filled him as he discovered that all the entrances to this building were locked up tight. Why that one in particular, he wondered as he stalked over to the last building. It was smaller than the others, occupying only thirty square feet at most. The only door to this one was also locked, but a low-hanging window had been busted out long ago, and he climbed inside, making a cursory sweep of the room to make sure it was empty.

Smashed bottles littered the floor, glass all over. There were empty beer and pop cans strewn about. Trash of all sorts and varieties decorated the inside of the shed-like structure. Garrett tried to watch his step as he rifled through the debris with the flashlight and his eyes. As he moved to the center of the room, his shoes crunched and crushed newspapers, cans, sandwich wrappers, cardboard, and Styrofoam containers. Yuck, he thought. When he'd been through the whole area and discovered zip, he left, cranky, tired, and uncertain as to what he was seeking.

He found no signs that anyone had been in the road, either, as he approached the hill that led to Matt's yard. The numerous trees covering the hill draped their branches overhead, dangling their leaves before him. Garrett let the flashlight wander over the dead leaves, sticks, and dirt that were piled up at the base of the hill, near the edge of the road. At last, the light caught something that did not belong in the natural rubble. He was skeptical at first, positive that it was more litter mixed in with fall's refuse, but it was his duty to check it out. His eyes widened as the light landed on something long, thin, and yellow. He bent down and palmed the item.

A length of rope, he realized. This wasn't proof of anything, but as he was about to stand up, he noticed something else a few feet away. He reached out for it. Grabbing it, he saw that it looked like a small telescope.

Curious, he put the scope up to his eye and gasped. He switched off the flashlight with shaking hands and peered at his surroundings through the scope. Everything turned green. So it's a night vision scope. He stuck the scope and the rope in his pocket. I'd better get back and make sure Matt's all right. He left via the alley this time and ran up the street. As he headed for the front porch, he paused. Then he walked out back and through the fence gate. The rope, he thought, I wonder. He dashed to the end of the yard and switched on the flashlight.

Aiming the light upward, he perused the trees. The beam glinted off something metallic. Garrett climbed over the fence and scaled the tree on which he'd glimpsed the object. He was able to extend his arm just enough to grab the thing. After shoving it in his other pocket, he slid down the trunk and hurried inside. He found Matt turned on his side, snoring, the blanket messed up in bunches between his legs. With a gentle smile, Garrett untangled the blanket, covered him again, and went to the kitchen to examine his find. He pulled the last item out of his pocket, turning it over in his hands. His suspicion was confirmed.

"A pulley. So that's how they got Buster in. But how'd they get the rope on and off him? Did he have some sort of removable harness? And that doesn't explain how come there were no footprints or paw prints on either side of the fence," he said, pondering aloud.

He shook his head in frustration and made a decision to keep the things he'd found on his person, lest they should disappear as had the fake dog. Back in the family room, he reclined in the easy chair and tried to sleep. As his eyes closed, Milo's face burst forth in his mind's eye. Milo, he thought, I'll do my best to make sure your future is a good one. He blinked. *I don't even know why I'm worried or what it is that could trap him. And how does Norm Morriston fit into this?* He was left with a sinking suspicion that he would find out sooner or later. A chill ran down his spine. *Oh God, please don't let anything happen to him,* he prayed. All at once, a serene reassurance that all was well flowed through him. At last, he was out.

Matt crashed awake. Groaning, he sat up, noticing something in his hand. *Where did this come from? And how'd this blanket get here?* His eyes adjusted to the darkness, and he saw Garrett asleep in the recliner. *Gar,* he realized. *Boy, he tucked this blanket in tight enough.* He struggled to free himself, musing, *I hope he doesn't tuck Milo in like this.* After he got loose, he went into the kitchen and stared at the clock on the oven. It was 6:45 a.m.

"Too early," he moaned as he went into the bathroom.

Once the light was on, he opened his palm and unfolded the piece of paper. His eyes blurred as he tried to focus on the words, but he was able to read what was written there.

"'Matt, going to the brickyard to check out a hunch. Locked the doors, but I took your key ring. Also, I left the floodlight on out back, so don't turn it off. P.S. Do not come after me if you wake up before I return. I'll be back soon, no fussing. Hugs and kisses, Gar.' That idiot," he muttered.

He threw the note in the garbage and trudged back to the family room, about to give Garrett a piece of his mind. He was stopped by the look on his friend's face. Gar wore a serene expression, but it gave him the gut-wrenching impression that this was the first bit of serenity Garrett had experienced in a while. *We'll discuss it when he gets up,* he decided. Then he noticed a piece of yellow rope hanging out of one of Gar's pockets. Both pockets appeared to hold something bulky. Gar's shirt covered up the top half of the pockets and anything that might be sticking out. Matt shrugged. *I'm not sure I even want to know,* he thought, lying on the couch once more.

At 8:10, Garrett awoke, rising with the eerie sensation that he was late for something important. He glanced at his watch and gaped. Time to leave. He raced out the front door, locking it behind him. Then he booked home and entered through his bedroom window. He checked his watch again. 8:35. Phew. Perfect timing. His parents got up around nine on Saturdays, so he was safe. He lay down, trying to drift off, but his eyes kept opening. I'm wide awake. He groaned. Why does that always happen when you're tired? Milo burst in at that exact moment. Garrett stifled a shriek. Milo's eyes widened. He appeared shocked to see Garrett.

"Oh, you're back. I dunno where you were, but I'm glad you got back before Mom and Dad got up. I was worried you'd get in trouble."

"Not to worry. That is, if you keep your mouth shut."

"Okay. But where'd you go?"

"Not that it concerns you, dear boy, but Matt required my help."

"Why?"

"That's definitely something that you don't need to know," he replied with a frown.

"How come?"

"Because it's none of your beeswax, that's why."

"Did Matt do something bad?"

"Where would you get an idea like that?"

Milo squinted at him. "Something funny's going on with everyone. You, Matt, Mom, and Dad. You're all being weird."

Garrett jumped. "What do you mean?"

"You and Matt act like you're freaked. And Mom and Dad are all weird, too."

Intrigued, he said, "Really? How do you mean?" So you noticed it as well, he thought.

"Last night, while you were on Facebook with your girlfriend," Milo began.

"You little spy!"

Milo stuck his tongue out in reply.

"You little twerp. Just try it again and see what happens," Garrett snapped, face turning red.

"Well you kept coming in on me when I was sick, so I figured I could check on you, too."

"Fine, get to the point."

"Well, Mom and Dad were watching TV, and they kept getting phone calls. And Daddy kept looking around all strange, like he didn't want someone to hear. And Momma kept looking at him with sad eyes."

"What do you mean sad eyes?"

"That's how she looked: sad. It was bizarro."

Garrett sighed, rubbing his chin. Hm, sad eyes. I wonder why she was sad. He almost jumped again when Milo grabbed his arm.

"Garrett, what's wrong?"

"Ugh. Nothing's wrong. I'm thinking."

"But you look so sad," he said.

"Not sad. Serious. Was this how Mom looked last night?"

Milo nodded.

"Well, don't worry. She was probably fretting over something ridiculous."

"Why would she do that?"

"Who knows. Mothers are weird."

Milo glared at him.

"What?"

"Don't call Mom weird."

"You just called her weird yourself."

"That was different. 'Sides, you're way more weird."

"Ooh, touche. Come here, you little brat," Garrett said, grabbing him. He pulled the protesting boy close and rubbed the top of his head with his fist.

"Ah. Stop it," Milo whined.

"Fine. Why don't you run along, then?"

"Don't tell me what to do," he pouted.

"I'm not. I'm simply telling you to vacate my room," Garrett corrected.

"Oh yeah? Well, what if I tell Mom you snuck out last night?"

"Yes, you could do that. And I could tell her about the three accidents you had last week. Which, if you'll recall, I cleaned up."

Milo blushed. "Okay. I won't say nothing."

"Anything, Milo."

"I don't understand how come you're always correcting me, but you get Cs in English."

"How do you know about that?"

"I heard Momma say so."

"Shouldn't you be leaving now?"

Milo giggled as he left the room. Sometimes he's really bloody annoying, Garrett thought. He decided he would ask if he could go to Matt's later. He wanted to share his discovery. Yawning, he stretched out again on his bed.

Matt roused himself at eleven and noticed that Garrett was gone. He found his key ring on the table and concluded that Gar had gone home to avoid getting in trouble. *Maybe I should go over there and see what he found.* He stretched. Suddenly, an idea came to him. He hurried upstairs to change his clothes. *If Gar can investigate on my behalf without my consent, then I can do the same for him.* He snatched his belt knife and slipped it into the pocket of his jeans. Then he retrieved his coat from the closet, pocketed his keys, and left for Richard Street.

Richard Street was a conundrum to the residents of Kangley. The road ran diagonally for a long stretch, then curved just a little ways after it intersected Monroe Street and went straight, paralleling Monroe. Everyone agreed that it was the oddest street in town and remained puzzled at its design. No one knew that at the time the road was paved, the town was much more spread out and haphazard. Back then, Richard Street ran parallel to a forest and skirted around a cornfield. There were no houses or streets nearby at that time. The road was the connecting feature between both parts of Kangley then. Now, however, it was relegated to a charming quirk in the town's layout.

As Matt approached the historic street, he gawked. What he saw caused him to stop dead. In front of him stood a white wolf. It was so still, he wasn't sure it was real until he locked eyes with it. The wolf stared at him in a casual, yet meaningful fashion. He swallowed hard. Part of him could see that the wolf was not a threat and meant him no harm. Though its eyes were trained on him, it was calm and docile. Yet he shuddered. He didn't care if his fear was rational or not, he just wished the wolf would run off.

Wolf or no wolf, I've got to scope out this street, he thought. He walked around the animal, giving it a wide berth. The wolf made no noise as it sauntered up to him. It jumped on him, pawing at him, tail wagging. Unable to cry out, Matt shoved the wolf away and continued forward. He wanted to run, but he figured that would agitate the beast. A light tug on his wrist stopped him again. He glanced over and saw that the wolf had hold of his wrist. It was tugging him, as if to pull him away from Richard Street. The wolf's jaws gripped him gently. It didn't hurt, though he could feel the teeth pressed against his skin. It was just enough to get his attention.

Matt's heart raced. He tried to pull his arm back enough to break the grip. The wolf tugged harder, yet it didn't hurt at all. Quaking, he turned to push the wolf's head back in an attempt to free his wrist again and let out a strangled cry. No longer was a wolf gripping his wrist. Now it was a white pit bull. I'm not seeing this. He shook his arm just as the dog opened its mouth and got free. Matt ran for all he was worth. If he didn't know any better, he'd think the dog had let him get away. A block down, he stopped to catch his breath and looked over his shoulder. The dog and the wolf were gone, as if they'd never been there at all.

"Will all this weirdness never end?" he muttered.

When he caught his breath, he continued down Richard Street. He made it about halfway up the diagonal portion of the road. So far, he had yet to see anything unusual, aside from the encounter with the wolf and the pit bull. Then something caught his eye. It was a large, three story home that used to be a bed and breakfast. The place towered above him. Its faded pea-green siding, tan shutters, and dark brown shingled roof were something to behold. The color scheme alone was enough to turn his stomach.

Around the sides and back of the property, a privacy fence had been put up. It had once been brown, but now the color was faded out. It seemed odd to him that this fence went around the sides and back of the lot, yet was open on both sides in the front, allowing him to see straight into the backyard.

He paused in front of the walk, recalling that the former Richard Street B&B had been converted to a home after business had plummeted in the early 90s. The old design had been much more appealing. He'd seen the picture in the paper when one of the local reporters had featured the B&B in the town history week edition. Then, it had been a cheerful, canary-yellow with light blue shutters and window trims and a blue-gray, tiled roof.

In the years since it closed, many families had come and gone in that house. Each had claimed the place was haunted, and it became vacant faster with each buyer. It had remained empty for the last decade. *Why don't they just tear this old beast down*, he thought, gazing at the boarded-up windows and the broken door. The lawn had been mowed not long ago, he saw, but weeds had overtaken the neglected flowerbeds. The porch steps were dilapidated and canting to one side. The screen door hung off its hinges. The once beautiful stained oak door behind it now featured a gaping hole through the center, where the diamond-shaped glass pane had been busted out.

It gave Matt the creeps just looking at it, and he was about to go on his way, when he noticed a white Chevy van parked near the garage in back. This shouldn't have bothered him, because it could've been someone working on the building or checking on things inside. However, the sight of that van made his heart pound. He dashed down the sidewalk, putting as much distance between himself and that house as he could. In his mad flight, he scanned both sides of the road, but there was nothing of further interest to him. He ran the rest of the way to Garrett's, panting.

Garrett slept until ten o'clock. When he awoke, his father was frowning at him from the doorway. He sat up, fear rising in his chest. Perhaps Milo had ratted him out.

"Garrett, why are you sleeping so late? You know I want everyone up for breakfast when I get up. Your mom tried waking you several times, but you wouldn't respond. We're a little concerned."

"Sorry, Dad. I had trouble sleeping last night. Last time I checked the clock, it was 8:35, and I figured I had time to snooze. I must've conked out."

"Oh? Were you staying up too late again?"

"No. I went to bed at midnight, and I did fall asleep, but I kept waking up every two hours."

"Are you troubled about something?"

"Not that I can think of." He scratched his head.

"You know you can talk to us, right?"

"Yeah. But there's nothing to talk about."

"Well, all right. But if you are in trouble, you tell us what's going on, understand?"

"Sure, Dad." Not on your life, he thought, embarrassed.

"Better get to the kitchen. We're ready to eat."

"Ooh, what're we having?"

"I talked your mother into steak and eggs, plus bacon and sausage."

"Will there be toast?"

His father rolled his eyes. "Of course."

"And Milo's not whining that he wants pancakes?"

"No. I told him we can have that tomorrow."

"Sweet."

By the time breakfast was over and cleaned up, it was eleven o'clock. Garrett noticed that his parents were wearing their fancy clothes. "What's up with you two?"

"We're going out for a while," said his mother.

"I'm assuming I have to babysit Milo."

"No. We're dropping him off at his friend Jason's to spend the night. So if you and Matt want to hang out, that's fine. But I need you to stay here until noon. I'm expecting a package, and someone has to sign for it," his father explained.

"Ooh, mysterious package. Could it contain objects, perhaps?"

"Don't get nosy," his dad scolded.

"Relax, Brandon. He was just joking," his wife replied.

"I'm perfectly relaxed, Gertrude. Make sure you stay near enough to hear the door, Garrett. Come along, Milo."

Garrett gawked at this exchange.

"I'm ready, Dad," Milo replied, lugging his backpack along.

After they left, he sat on the couch and called Matt. He intended to let Matt know he'd be over as soon as he was done waiting on the package. No one answered. He glanced at his watch. It was 11:07. Odd. Matt's usually up by now, he thought as he flipped on the TV. His search through the guide revealed that nothing interesting was on. There never is. He brought up the DVR listings and groaned. There was nothing of interest recorded either. Desperate, he played one of his mother's recordings, an episode of the old series *Murder, She Wrote*.

"Ah, Jessica Fletcher. Beats *NCIS*. Ugh, the lame acting, yet fun plots that don't require much thought. Those were the days: *before* I was born, mind you." Who am I talking to, he wondered.

He was really involved in the show when the doorbell rang. He paused the TV and checked his watch. 11:35. Must be Fed Ex or UPS. He opened the door to see Matt struggling for breath.

"Hi, Gar, can I come in?"

"Matt? You're not UPS or Fed Ex. Shame on you. Why're you all sweaty and out of breath?"

"I had to run," Matt began.

"Aw, so sweet. You missed me. I missed you too," he said with a smart alec grin.

Matt glared at him as he entered, catching his breath. When he was able to speak, he said, "Not because of you. I'll explain later. Right now, I want to know what you found down at the brickyard last night."

"You know about that? How? Did you develop psychic powers or telepathy while I was unawares?"

Matt rolled his eyes. "You left me a note, duh."

"Oh, heh, that. Yeah, I kinda forgot about that." Garrett laughed.

"So show me what you found."

"Later. I've got to wait for a package that my dad needs me to sign for."

"Okay. So where is everyone?"

Garrett shrugged. "Mom and Dad went somewhere. Milo's staying the night at a friend's, and I was gonna come over to your house as soon as the package came."

"I see. Oh, I have a question."

"Shoot."

"Did you have to tuck me in last night?"

"Wait, what? Tuck you in? What are you talking about?"

"This morning, I had to fight my way free of the blanket you tucked me in with." Matt blushed. *This is humiliating, and saying it out loud makes it even worse*, he thought.

"Dude, I didn't tuck you in. I simply covered you with a blanket. It's not my fault you move around so bloody much in your sleep."

Matt's blush deepened.

Garrett pretended not to notice. "Sit, Matthew, and we shall see what Jessica discovers next."

"Who?"

"Jessica Fletcher, otherwise known as J.B. Fletcher," he responded.

"*Murder, She Wrote*, dude? Seriously?"

"So bloody what. There's nothing else on."

"Okay. I guess it's not that lame. Besides, I don't mind Angela Lansbury."

"There ya go; that's the spirit. My thoughts exactly." Garrett hit the play button.

A few minutes later, the package arrived. Garrett paused the show, signed for the package, and set it on the table. He returned to the couch and grabbed the remote.

"You gonna show me that stuff now?" Matt asked.

"But I want to see the end of this," he whined.

"Oh, fine," Matt retorted, uttering an annoyed sigh.

They finished the episode, and Matt was about to get up, when he realized that Garrett was rewinding the episode to the beginning.

"What are you doing?"

"Rewinding it, duh."

"But you can just start it over."

"I know. I will do that when I'm done."

"Don't even tell me you missed something and you're going back to figure it out."

"No. I just wanna hear the theme song again."

"Why?"

"Because it's awesome. Don't you just love that music?" he said as he played it. "It's all intriguey and stuff."

"You are maddening."

"Oh, come on. It's not that long. Show some couth."

"Oh, for goodness' sake," Matt muttered.

They listened to the theme one more time, with Garrett humming along. Matt groaned.

"Oh, all right, Mr. Whinypants, follow me." He led the way to his room and took the items from his dresser drawer, displaying them for Matt.

"And you found these at the brickyard? Where?" His eyes were wide.

"The night vision scope—that's what it is—I found along with the rope at the bottom of the hill behind your house. The pulley I found up on a tree branch near the back of the fence."

Alarmed, Matt cried, "Then that means…"

"Yes. They used the pulley to lower Buster into the yard."

"But I never saw a harness on him."

"I know. Ooh, maybe they had a camo-harness on him, covered with synthetic fur like on the fake dog."

"But how would they detach and reattach the harness?"

"Maybe they didn't. Maybe they used a long enough rope that he could move around freely."

"I would have seen the rope."

"Mm, yes. Okay, perhaps they had some sort of remote controlled detaching/reattaching harness."

"That aside, how come there were no tracks in the snow, when someone had to handle Buster and manage the pulley from behind the fence?"

"Yes, that one is troublesome. It's not like they could have used a painted canvass stretched across the snow to make it appear untouched, because we walked on the snow ourselves. Since we're sure numerous individuals are working on this, perhaps they had a large reserve of snow and somehow filled in their tracks and evened it out when they were done."

"That would be hard to manage, but I guess it could be done somehow."

"Well, if not, at least we know I have a good imagination."

"Of a deviant sort," Matt quipped.

"True enough. Anyway, I believe whoever was going to threaten you this morning dropped the scope when Buster began barking."

"What about the rope and the pulley?"

"Sloppy clean up, or they planned to use the pulley again to lower Buster into the yard."

"Man, not only is this insane, but I don't feel safe at all."

"Don't worry, Matt. We've got some sort of spirit soldier to help us now."

"That's sort of comforting."

"So, tell me, what were you running from when you came to the door?"

"Well, it may be nothing, but I was on my way here, so—"

"Don't tell me you went down Richard Street," Garrett interrupted.

"I did," Matt returned with a curt nod.

"Matt, spirit soldier man said we shouldn't go down there."

"No, he said you shouldn't. Although, I think you're right that we should both avoid using that road."

"What happened?"

"I decided that since you went prowling about the brickyard without me, I would explore Richard Street for you."

"Don't take risks like that, Matt."

"Hey, don't scold me. You're the one that went to the brickyard in the middle of the night alone."

"I knew—or, at least, was relatively positive—that no one was down there."

"Can I continue?"

"I don't know, can you?"

"May I?"

"Be my guest."

"So, as I was approaching Richard Street, I see this wolf. A white wolf."

"Wait, what?"

"There was a white wolf standing on the corner, just staring at me. And I tried to walk around it."

"Wait, hold up. You see a wolf, and instead of running the other way, you're like, 'Oh, I'll just walk around. My bad, wolf.'?"

"I needed to go that way, so I had to pass the wolf. And I did, but then it followed me and jumped on me. I pushed it away, and it grabbed me by the wrist as I was turning. I didn't even realize it until I felt a tug on my arm. I look, and it's pulling my arm lightly, like it's trying to pull me back the way I came. I tried to shake free, and I looked away for a sec, then my arm gets tugged again. So now I'm yanking my arm back, and I see that it's no longer a wolf that's got me."

"What do you mean?"

"It was a white pit bull. The wolf was gone."

"Uh-huh," Garrett said. "Go on."

"So I finally got free, and I bolted. When I stopped to catch my breath, I looked back, and the dog was gone too."

"Creepy."

"So then I'm walking along, not seeing anything of interest, when I came to this house. You know, the old bed and breakfast?"

"Ah, yes. I seem to recall that. The incredibly conspicuous green house."

"That's the one. So I'm staring at it, and I noticed that out back by the garage, a white van was parked. It gave me a bad vibe, so I ran off. That's the only thing I saw that made me uneasy."

"With the possible exception of the wolf and the pit bull?"

"Well, obviously."

"Spooky."

"What do you think?"

"I don't know yet. But there is something that concerns me around this domicile."

"What do you mean?"

"Milo caught me sneaking in, and he said something about everyone acting weird."

"He did? What'd he mean?"

"He said you and I were freaked out, and Mom and Dad were getting phone calls last night while I was in my room. Apparently, Dad kept looking around like he didn't want someone listening. Then they tell me they're going out today, but don't tell me where or why, and they were all dressed up. Then they take Milo with them so he can spend the night at his friend's house. Oh, and Dad got all jumpy when I made a joke about what might be in his package and told me not to snoop."

"And you think that this is all connected to that funeral business?"

"Yes."

"It is kind of suspicious."

"It's out of character. And worse, Milo notices all of this."

"That is distressing."

"You know what else is odd?"

"What?"

"I was gonna ask Mom if I could come over, but I got distracted. Right before they left, Dad said if you and I wanted to hang out, it was okay. I know we hang out a lot, but I find their sudden attentiveness to you a bit disconcerting."

"Okay, that combined with everything else is definitely beserko."

"No kidding, Sherlock."

"Grumpy?"

"Possibly. You know how I am when I don't get my beauty sleep."

Matt hid a smile with his hand. "So what do we do now?"

"Mm. Let us grab a soda and commence gaming."

"You don't want to go check out that B&B on Richard Street?"

"No. I'll take the warning of a ghost soldier seriously, for once in my life."

Matt noticed that he paled as he said this. "We could finish that commentary you've been working on."

"Excellent. Come, Matthew, to the kitchen."

They retrieved two sodas and retreated back to his room. As he opened the door, the hair stood up on the back of Garrett's neck. His breathing grew very shallow.

"What's wrong, Gar?"

"I don't know," he croaked.

The door swung in, and there, sitting on his bed, was the soldier from earlier in the morning. Gar's heart leapt into his throat. He turned to see if Matt was seeing this. Matt's eyes bugged out, his mouth dropped open.

"Garrett," said the soldier.

"Who the bloody heck are you?" he muttered.

"It's not important right now. You did well earlier, but both of you must stay away from the B&B, and do not go down Richard Street again. Let the monsters of the past remain buried, and keep away from the monsters of the present."

Before Garrett could answer, Matt asked, "Why?"

"It's too dangerous for you handle."

"Does all this have to do with what's happening to Matt?"

"Yes. But both of you are at risk."

"Okay, so we'll avoid Richard Street," Matt assured him.

"You two must leave right away. Go, take the back alley down to the next street and then walk to the highway. From there, go back to Matt's. You're not safe here right now."

They wanted to ask more, but the soldier faded away.

"We'd better go," Garrett said. He grabbed his cell phone and keys while Matt snatched up the pulley, rope, and scope.

They left by the back door, hurried through the backyard to the alley, following the soldier's instructions to a tee, and arrived at Matt's forty minutes later.

Tangled Ropes of Destiny

"Seeing as we had to retreat here, do you want me to show you where I found that stuff?" Garrett asked, pointing at the things in Matt's hands.

"In a bit."

"In a bit? Usually, you're all gung-ho to explore. What's up?"

"I'm starving. There's some stroganoff in the fridge with my name on it."

Garrett looked at him, befuddled. "You didn't eat before you came to my house?"

"Nah. Besides, you're a better cook than I am."

He rolled his eyes. "I'm not your personal chef, Matt."

Matt raised his eyebrows and grinned. "That's what my mom says."

"Ugh, typical teenage boys," muttered Garrett.

He snickered and fixed himself a plate. "You want some?"

"Later. I must confess, I had breakfast not long before you arrived."

"That late? Don't you guys always eat by ten?"

"Yes, but I overslept. I awoke to see Father peering at me. He became worried and lectured me about how I could talk to him if something was bothering me. He also gave me the third degree about sleeping in. I panicked at first, thinking Milo had ratted on me."

"Man, I hate it when they give you those lectures."

"Meh, I understand it, but still: lame."

"Just think, someday we'll be doing that to our kids."

"Don't you need to find a mate first?" Gar teased.

"My life's complicated enough as it is."

"True, indeed."

"Can—May I eat now?"

"Yes, you may."

Matt dug in as Garrett puzzled over the irony that they had fled his house because it was unsafe, only to be instructed to come back here. Well, now I know how a ping pong ball feels, he thought. When Matt finished eating, he soaked the dishes, and they went out back. Garrett pointed to the tree he'd climbed the night before.

"That's where the pulley was hanging."

"Hey, look. What's that white thing at the base of the tree?"

Garrett squinted. "Looks like more rope. So, the plot thickens."

"What do you mean?"

"I got to thinking on the way here, and I realized that this thin piece of yellow rope is not strong enough to hold Buster's weight. But this white one is a tow rope. That would support Buster no problem, and it would've blended in with the snow from a distance."

"So then, what was the yellow rope for?"

"That's what I'm wondering about."

"Do you think it was just incidental garbage? Or did they actually use it for something else?"

"Your guess is as good as mine. Why don't we go down to the brickyard and have a look around where I found this? You wanted to go there, anyway."

"Yeah, let's go."

When they reached the spot where he'd found the scope and the yellow rope, Garrett pointed at the small amount of liter. "I found that stuff right here."

"So you found them together?"

"No. I found the rope first. The scope was a few feet away."

"I guess the rope could've been part of the debris."

"We can never be sure. But I really believe this rope is just as significant as the white one."

"Think so? Hm." Matt paused. "Something just occurred to me. Let me see that pulley again."

"Okay, but why?" he asked as he handed it over.

Matt eyed the pulley for a moment, comparing it with the white rope. "Just as I thought. This tow rope is way too big to fit on this pulley."

Garrett gawked at him. "Then what was it used for? And what did they use to haul Buster up with? Because, I'm telling you, that yellow rope would have snapped."

Matt sighed. "I don't know what to think anymore."

"I'm out of ideas, too. Maybe we should go back to the house and take a break from thinking for now."

"Are we even safe there?"

"According to the ghost soldier, we're safer here than at my house."

"I suppose. So what game do you wanna play?"

"My mind is frazzled. I can't focus enough to game right now. Maybe I'll just watch you."

"You can snooze while I play if you want. But what game do you wanna watch? And I swear if you even suggest the Barbie game, you're dead."

"Then why do you have it?" asked Garrett.

"It's for my little cousin Stacy when she comes over."

"Darn. That's a really fun one, too. All right, what about Final Fantasy?"

"That's doable."

Garrett smirked as Matt went to fetch the game. He had no idea that the real reason he'd received a Barbie game last Christmas was because his mom made the mistake of asking Garrett for suggestions on what kind of games he was interested in. Garrett snickered as he thought of the look on her face when she'd said, "And you're sure he wants a Barbie video game? I never thought he'd ask for something like that. Although, I suppose it would be cute if he and Stacy played it together when she's over."

"What's so funny?" Matt asked when he returned.

"Nothing. I was thinking of my hijinks in Brandenburg's class, that's all," he lied.

"You gotta stop that. Unless you want to 'become more intimate' with him in your off time."

"Ew. That's every high school student's worst fear. Except mine."

Matt eyed him curiously, and Garrett responded, "Well, it isn't. Toilet monsters. Now, there's a worst fear for ya."

Rolling his eyes, Matt put the game in the console. Garrett lounged on the couch. His eyes grew heavy, and his head lolled to the side as he drifted away. When he was asleep, Matt covered him up and turned off the PlayStation. He wasn't in the mood for games, either. Not after the bender he'd had last night. *I am so bored*, he thought. He was too lazy to watch a movie, and he didn't want to leave Gar down here alone. He snapped his fingers and ran upstairs to get his keyboard.

For a moment, he couldn't think of anything to play. He settled for a bit of score and a few songs from *The Lion King* soundtrack. Then he moved on to animated movie scores composed by James Horner. He kept the volume low and stayed in the living room so as not to disturb Gar. He wasn't sure why he liked animated movie scores so much, but the music spoke to him.

He grinned from ear to ear as his fingers stretched across the keys. Time passed swifter than he realized. He looked up at the clock with a start when it got too dark for him to see without a light. *Holy smoke, it's already four o'clock.* Gar had been asleep for about three hours. Matt got up to check on him. He was still conked out on the couch, and Matt couldn't help smiling. Garrett looked almost adorable, lying on his back, his mouth hanging open. Soft, low breaths escaped him. Every now and then, his feet would twitch. Matt put a hand over his mouth to keep from laughing. His feet twitch like a dog's. He must be worn out, because he's not even talking in his sleep, he observed.

With that, he stretched and went back to playing. Every so often, he got the itch to play like crazy. Marathon keyboarding, he called it. This time, he chose music a bit more modern. He beat out some rock and pop songs, singing along. His singing left something to be desired, but he enjoyed singing, even if he wasn't great at it. Soon, he felt a hand on his shoulder. He shrieked.

"Sorry, Matt, didn't mean to scare you."

"Gar, you're awake. You want some stroganoff now?"

"Yes. But you didn't have to stop your lovely show on my account. I would've helped myself when I was ready."

"I wouldn't have stopped if you hadn't scared the daylights out of me," Matt grumbled.

"I apologize."

"You should've let me know you were awake so I could've stopped singing."

"Come on, you're not that bad. I kind of enjoyed it. You'll never be a professional singer, but you're not so bad that it makes my ears bleed."

"Thanks. I think."

"Dinner?"

"I thought you were gonna help yourself?"

"Oh come on, I waited on you twice."

"Fine. Let me get your dinner ready."

"Yay. Mattie, that would be so awesome. Thank you."

"Smart mouth," he retorted.

"Would you really want it any other way? Think of how utterly horrifying that would be: a well-mannered, tactful Gar. Blah. It's enough to make your skin crawl."

Matt declined to answer his query. He fixed a heaping plate of stroganoff. Garrett scarfed it down with gusto.

"For store bought crap, this isn't too bad. You're a better cook than I realized. Or did the glove do all the work?"

"The what?"

"The glove on the box, Einstein."

"Very funny."

"Thanks, I thought so."

Matt was about to respond, when Garrett's cell phone rang.

"Hello," Garrett said.

"Hi, son. You're not at home, are you?"

"Hi, Mom. I'm at Matt's. Do you need me to come home?"

"Oh, no. Go ahead and stay at Matt's tonight. Don't worry about getting home early tomorrow, either. We got caught up with something, so we're not going to be home until tomorrow afternoon."

"Caught up with what?"

"That doesn't concern you. Oh, your father wants to know if the package came today."

"Yeah. I signed for it, just like he asked."

"Okay, good. Well, we're on the road, so I better let you go."

"Wait, what about Milo?"

"What about him?"

"What time is he supposed to be home tomorrow? Do I need to go get him?"

"No. We'll pick him up on our way home. You just stay there with Matt and have fun."

"Uh, okay. Anything else?"

"No, that's it. I love you."

"I love you, too, Mom." He hung up. He held the phone in his hand and stared at it for a moment.

"You look troubled. What is it?" Matt asked.

"My mother just asked if I was at home, and when I told her I was here, she said I should spend the night and have fun. She asked me right off the bat if I was at home. I wonder if she's aware of the danger at our house. But how could she know that? And why is she so eager to keep the two of us together, away from the house?"

"Man, this just gets weirder and weirder."

"I'm really freaked," he confessed.

"What else did she say?"

"She said she and Dad won't be home until tomorrow afternoon and that I shouldn't worry about being home early tomorrow. Then she added that they got caught up with something."

"Caught up with what?"

"I don't know. She pretty much told me to butt out, that it's none of my business."

"Okay, I think you were right about something being up with them. I'm sorry I doubted you."

"It's all right. But I didn't even bring a change of clothes. Let alone a toothbrush."

"We have a ton of extra toothbrushes. My dad buys them in bulk. You can use one of those. As for clothes, you can wear some of mine."

"Thanks, bro."

"Any time."

Garrett rolled his eyes. "I was being sarcastic. You're shorter than me, remember?"

"Oh yeah. Well, you might be able to wear my P.E. shorts. They're clean."

"No way," Garrett muttered.

"Okay. I guess you could borrow my dad's robe, and I'll wash your clothes."

"Ordinarily, I'd say no, but as it's not safe to go home, I guess I have no choice."

"That settles it then."

"Bloody Matt. Still, it beats having to wear your mother's nightgown."

Matt cast a strange look at him.

"Don't get cute. I was only trying to be funny." Garrett finished his meal and took the dishes to the sink. Then he opened the dishwasher and took out the few dishes that were inside.

"What are you doing?" Matt asked.

"I'm gonna wash these. Might as well get them all. There's not that many."

"You don't have to do that."

"Meh, I'm used to it. Besides, you cooked the food and prepared me a plate. It's an unspoken rule at our house that whoever cooks doesn't have to do dishes. Whoever cleans his plate but does not sully his hands cooking must clean up everything while the cook relaxes."

"I see. I'm just used to doing them all the time."

"Ah, but see, it's always fun to watch Milo and Dad clean up when I make the meal. Of course, Mom gets a pass, since she cleans everything else."

"Cool."

Garrett washed the dishes, while Matt dried and put them away. When they finished, Matt said, "What do you suppose could have kept your parents away for the night?"

"I don't know. I have no idea where they are."

"You still freaked out?"

"Yeah. I wish I knew what was going on."

"What if we watch a movie or something? That might distract you for a little bit."

"No. I don't really want to do anything right now. I just can't help thinking," he paused.

"What is it?"

"I'm just happy Milo's not home, since we were warned that it's not safe."

"Yeah, good thing he went to his friend's."

"If that's where he went," Garrett added.

Matt gasped. "What are you getting at?"

"I'm not sure. It just came out."

"Where else could he be?"

"I dunno. The hospital, perhaps."

"Huh? Why?"

"Maybe he's sicker than I've been led to believe."

"Psh, come on. Think, Gar. He went to school, and he was fine."

"He did look much better," Garrett conceded.

"Then why are you so worried about his health?"

"I don't know. I'm not sure where this concern is coming from. It just seems strange to me that the day after Milo is able to go back to school, he gets to go spend the night at a friend's. Especially given how fretful Mom's been over him."

"That is a tad odd. Look, maybe we're reading too much into things. You know what? Let's watch some TV. It's got to be better than idle speculation."

"Yeah, unless you're in politics or one of those analysts," he murmured.

Matt's skin crawled, and a scratchy sensation flared up in the back of his throat. Norm Morriston's face glared at him from the confines of his mind. He shuddered as he turned on the television and flipped through the guide. A minute or so later, he uttered a protracted groan.

"Why isn't there ever anything on?"

"Now you know why I settled for *Murder, She Wrote*."

"Yeah, I wish we had that option right now."

"Hey, hold on. Scroll back up, Matt."

"See something good?"

"No. Go back to that talk show there. See the description?"

"Up and coming singer Newsome Jones performs," Matt read.

"Not that. Look at the guests."

"Colin Segwick, Jason Thomas, and Norm Morriston," he said, choking on the congressman's name.

"Exactly. Change to that. Let us see what he has to say."

Matt clicked on *The Harrison Daniels Show*. Who is Harrison Daniels, and why does he have a talk show, he wondered, pausing the show.

"Why're you pausing it?"

"So you can change into Dad's robe, and I can start your laundry."

"Fine, might as well."

Garrett trotted up to retrieve the robe that he knew would be hanging on the bedpost in Matt's parents' room. I hope this has been washed recently, he thought as he undressed and pulled the robe on. He stepped on the bottom of the robe, which was a little long on him, and stumbled about for a moment. Although he managed to steady himself, his heart lurched in his chest. His eyes were trained on the former deck door. It was ajar. The door was only open a sliver, but he noticed. Maybe the Marshalls' forgot to close it all the way before they left, he thought. But he knew Matt had searched the house a few times and would have rectified this if he had seen it. He was almost obsessive in his habits. There was no chance this had gone unnoticed. Garrett would have written this off if it had been anyone else, but Matt was way too fastidious.

Trembling, he tiptoed to the door, hoping Matt wouldn't hear his footsteps from below. Then he pushed the door shut and engaged the deadbolt. After a frantic look around, he paused to sense the air. There didn't seem to be any immediate danger. He calmed himself by reasoning that the ghost soldier had assured them they would be safe here. Or at least, he had implied it. Swallowing hard, he closed the robe around himself and tied the belt in a knot. Don't upset him with this tonight, he told himself and carried his clothes downstairs, handing them to Matt.

"Here you are, Mumsy," he joked.

Matt rolled his eyes. "Don't you think that's ironic, coming from the M.O.M. himself?"

"Perhaps."

At last, they settled down to watch the show. Both of them tuned out until they heard Harrison say, "Our next guest is a freshman in Congress who's making waves in the name of progress. He's also seeking re-election in Indiana this year. Please welcome Norman Morriston."

Norm Morriston entered with a smile plastered on his face. His brown hair was slicked back, and he wore a tan suit with shiny, black loafers. A pale blue dress shirt was revealed underneath his suit jacket, though he was not wearing a tie. He gave a little wave to the audience before he shook Harrison's hand and sat down.

"Welcome, Congressman Morriston. Glad to have you on the show," Harrison greeted.

Norm's gray eyes sparkled with annoyance. "Thanks, Harrison. By the way, I'm just good ole Norm. There's no need for formality." The condescending undertone in his voice made the boys cringe. His gaze, caught in close up by the camera, wrenched an involuntary shiver from Matt. The hair on their arms stood up.

"Norm it is, then. So I hear you've been making some waves lately over the budget proposal from Congressman Dupont. What exactly is it that has you so up in arms about the Dupont budget?"

"That's a great question, and I'm glad you asked," Norm stated, his cool smile thawing a few degrees. "You see, the Dupont budget purports to be a fair and swift, surefire answer to our current economic crisis. But the reforms are too drastic. We can't cut spending when America is out of work. Americans need…"

Matt didn't hear the rest, because Garrett retorted, "Uh, genius, if America has no jobs, how can anyone afford to pay taxes? If they can't afford to pay taxes, how in bloody heck can you dolts keep on spending? And how would getting us deeper in debt help us get out of debt and create jobs? That makes no sense."

Matt grinned. *Gar's fired up now. Prepare for a feisty speech.*

Meanwhile, Garrett glared at the television screen. "This guy really irks me. His suggestion isn't even a solution; it's sheer irresponsibility. He's as out of touch, inept, and corrupt as the rest of these politicians in Washington."

"I agree, but can you pipe down a moment and listen? I thought you wanted to hear what he had to say."

"I do. No, don't rewind it. We already know he's a buffoon."

Matt ignored him and rewound it anyway. *Ah, so we didn't miss anything: he is that predictable. I should have known by his intro that he'd blather on about how we need even more government spending,* he thought.

After Norm's statement, which seemed to go over the oblivious host's head, Harrison said, "I see. So Norm, now for the burning question. Is there a current or future Mrs. Morriston? All the ladies seem to comment on is how handsome you are. So I thought we'd do our female audience a favor and ask."

Matt and Garrett gawked at the TV. The remote dropped from Matt's hand. Liz would kick Harrison's butt for asking a dumb question like that, Garrett thought.

"No, not yet. Hopefully, I'll find the right woman soon. A good man always needs a good woman behind him." Norm chuckled.

"A good man my foot," Garrett muttered. "That's it, if he was here right now, I'd use a melee attack on him."

Matt didn't reply.

"One last question, Norm. Who do you like in tomorrow's football game?"

"I don't know. I'm a baseball fan, myself. It is America's pastime." He cheered the audience with a beatific smile.

"There you have it, ladies and gentlemen. Norm Morriston," Harrison announced.

"Are you serious? They just let him have a pass. There wasn't one hardball or provoking question. It was all drivel, except the obligatory budget question, thrown in to make him look good. He never even offered a counter-proposal or said what he thought the solution was, other than spend more, spend more," Garrett griped.

"I know it's not a news show, but really, what is the point of having a member of Congress on, if not to ask serious questions? Who actually enjoys watching showboating politicians?" Matt asked.

"No kidding, man. Perhaps zombie aliens have stolen their brains as well."

"Yeah, but it was like that last week when I saw him on the news, too. No one seems to ask him any difficult questions."

"Nor any adult questions. So it's not just the population of Tampa," Garrett added.

Matt gawked at him. "Wait, Tampa?"

"Yeah, the show is filmed in Tampa. Didn't you see that when we were reading the menu description?"

"No."

"So what's the big deal about that, anyway?" Garrett inquired, yawning.

"Dude, that's where my parents are," he croaked.

"Oh."

Suddenly, it dawned on Matt that his parents had been gone for over a week and hadn't called him once. His heart did a little flip. He grabbed the phone.

"You're gonna call them right now?" Gar asked.

Matt nodded. He tried his Mom's phone first. It rang until he got her voicemail. He hung up and dialed his father's cell number. This time, the call went straight to voicemail. Grunting and muttering under his breath, he decided to leave a message. The tone beeped, but as he opened his mouth to speak, a sound rendered him silent. He closed his mouth. Someone was breathing on the other end of the line. Straining his ears, he listened for any other sounds. For a moment, the breathing stopped, and all was quiet. Matt again opened his mouth to speak, but he was cut off.

"We have eyes," someone rasped.

A chill slithered down his spine. The raspy voice was followed by an audible click. How is that even possible when I'm on voicemail, Matt wondered. He waited a few moments and, hearing nothing further, left his message.

"Hey, Dad, just wondering if you guys are having fun. Don't forget to bring me back a cool souvenir. Okay, love you guys. Bye." As he was saying this, his voice became high-pitched, for in the background, he noticed beeping, followed by a whirring noise and the distinct sound of static. An acute sense of dread flooded him as he hung up the phone.

Garrett stared at him, very pale. "What happened?"

"Someone was breathing on the line and spoke to me and then I heard a click. And when I left my message, I heard these strange noises, plus static."

"Uh, that isn't odd at all. Nope. We've just entered a spy novel or something. That's all. Could you hear what was said?" he asked.

"Yes."

"Well?"

"He—I think it was a he—said, 'We have eyes.'"

Garrett shuddered but added, "Big deal, so do I. In fact, I have two. Or was it three? I can never remember."

"Not funny. How can you make jokes at a time like this?" scolded Matt.

"What do you propose we do, stand here and wet our pants?"

"I don't know what we should do. Does anyone ever really know what to do?"

"I'm sure there's a doomsday prepper out there somewhere who's prepared for this exact situation."

"Yeah, but we're not survivalists."

"We could be. Anyone can learn to survive."

"I suppose."

"Even Brandenburg," Garrett interjected with glee.

"Somehow I have my doubts about that."

Gar was quiet for a few seconds then added, "Mm, yes. He can be taught—or trained. All we'd need is a shock collar."

"That's cruel, even for you. Brandenburg doesn't deserve that."

"Not him. I was referring to Morriston."

"I'll agree with you there," Matt stated.

"I knew sooner or later you'd see things my way. Muahaha."

"Stop joking around. We need to figure out what we should do."

"I beg your pardon. How are we supposed to do anything? We only have a vague notion of what's going on."

"We need to go on the offensive," Matt insisted.

"Yeah, that'll happen. You become a martial arts master all of a sudden, Mattie?"

"Gar, I'm serious. We have to end this."

"How?"

He threw his hands up, groaning. "I don't know," he snapped.

"Dial it down a bit, man."

Matt glared at him, and Garrett looked away. His gaze softened. We are in way over our heads, he thought.

"Why don't we step outside for a minute?" Garrett suggested.

"Yeah, why not?" Matt paused when they got to the front door.

"What is it?"

"Wait here. I'm gonna go get my belt knife. You want a weapon to carry on you?"

"You're getting a weapon? We're only going out on the front porch. Is this what we've come to?"

Matt shrugged. "Better safe than sorry."

"Point taken. I'm proud of you, Matt. Way to go, thinking of our safety like that. Hooray."

"Shut it. Do you want a weapon or not?"

"Yeah. A sword would be nice. Or a rocket launcher. Do you have another knife?"

"No, but we'll borrow my dad's hunting knife."

"I didn't know he hunted."

"He doesn't."

"Then why does he—you know what? Never mind. I don't even care at this point."

Matt came down a few moments later and handed Gar a knife. Once outside, they stood on the porch, staring out at the street, entertaining their own observations. The crispness of the evening inspired Matt to consider the essence of the season.

Quiet nights, trees rustling and swaying in the breeze as they drop their orange and brown leaves. The smell of smoke from leaves burning in the fire makes for a satisfying sense of accomplishment, because one chore is done, at least for a while. Children are inside, cozy and warm. The air is fresh with a slight chill, making one long for a hoodie or a sweater. An explicit excitement is everywhere among the kids as they await Halloween, some for mischief, others for treats and thrills. Soon we'll be seeing pumpkins galore, all decked out and carved, he thought, a smile playing at the corners of his mouth.

Ah, fall. With all these shadowy areas and the lack of working streetlights, this would be a good setting for a Resident Evil game or movie, Garrett mused, looking up and down the street. Bloodthirsty zombies roaming about, clothes tattered and smeared with gore. The shotgun-wielding protagonist busting down doors and bursting through the houses in shameless yet dutiful exploration, possibly kicking in locked doors with awesome grit. Windows being bashed in as undead freaks attempt to enter barred areas, widening their domain. He practically drooled over the thought. But soon, unease drifted over him. He glanced around the neighborhood, surveying everything again.

And all at once, his delightful fantasy of hokey, Halloween-esque joy evaporated as adult practicality set in. With a gasp, it occurred to him that the shadows could hide not only zombie intruders, wary survivors, and heroes, but something else. Watchers, perhaps, could be lurking in the darkness with less scrupulous intentions than even the zombies. He began to imagine the lady across the street coming out to her car early in the morning. She'd be just about to leave for work, when bam, a masked man approached, knife or gun in hand. Garrett managed to stifle the rest of this image. What is wrong with me, picturing something like that, he wondered. Although with the economy as bad as it is, I wouldn't rule it out.

Matt's reverie broke when he saw Garrett twitch. "What is it, Gar?"

"Nothing. You know me and my stupid thoughts."

Matt rolled his eyes, but said, "You sure you're okay?"

"Fine." Garrett looked around for something to comment on to change the subject. His eyes fell on Mr. Welker's basement window. The light was on. "Hey, what do you suppose Welker's up to down there?" he asked, nodding toward the window.

"I don't know. Three or four nights a week he's down there, puttering around. Mom and I have wondered what he does down there for a while."

"Maybe he's got a hydroponic garden," Garrett suggested.

"Could be. But he goes down there for hours, almost always at night."

"Do you suppose he could be an inventor?"

"I guess it's possible. If he is, I hope he invents something good."

"I hope he invents a way to keep your pillow cold without hassle."

Matt gaped at him. "That's what you come up with?"

"Hey, it's something people would want," he insisted.

"I guess."

"See? Being an entrepreneur isn't so hard."

"You still have to come up with a way to make it work. And a cost-effective way to mass produce and market it."

"Not according to the president," Garrett joked.

"Don't even get me started on that," Matt said with a glower.

"Sorry. I know your parents were pretty miffed over that comment."

"You bet they were. They've busted their humps for years to get their business off the ground and to be successful. There are times when I barely see them because they're working so hard."

"Same with my parents, especially Dad. He's worked tons of overtime."

"Things okay at the factory?"

"So far, yeah. Being a supervisor has saved his job, but the company keeps laying off because of the economy."

"What about your mom?" Matt inquired.

"Her job's safe for now. Though she has to commute four times a week to the city, and the gas prices are killing them."

"I bet. What does she do again?"

"She's in accounts management for Herrington National."

"Is that the bank I keep seeing ads for? The one that charges no fees?"

"Yep, that's the one."

"Cool. But I'll bet that's a stressful job."

"Fortunately, she has me to ease the tension."

"Because you're so good at that," Matt added with a smirk.

"That I am, Mattie. Take you, for example. You'd be curled up in a neurotic ball of fear if I weren't here."

Matt huffed. Garrett gaped at him and pointed at his face, inhaling sharply.

"What is it?" Matt asked, heart thudding away.

"I'll be buggered. Matt, did you know that you also have two eyes? Is that normal?"

Matt shook a fist at him. "You're gonna get socked, if you don't knock it off."

Garrett pouted and muttered, "Fine. I'll behave."

"Have you had enough fresh air now? Can we go in?"

"That's a good idea, since I am only wearing a robe. We wouldn't want to inadvertently shock the Hollands, should they be out and about for their nightly walk."

Matt started laughing. They went inside, and he threw the laundry in the dryer. Then they agreed to brawl each other in the latest Mortal Kombat game. After three hours of gruesome finishers, Matt finished Garrett's laundry, and they called it a night. Garrett chuckled to himself. *How ironic is it that I'm getting dressed just to go to bed?* He covered his mouth, but it was too late. A burst of giggles came wheezing out.

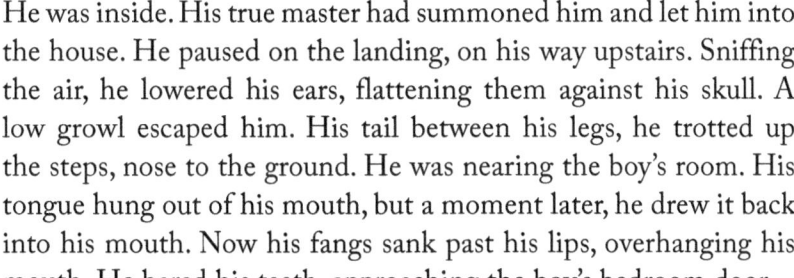

He was inside. His true master had summoned him and let him into the house. He paused on the landing, on his way upstairs. Sniffing the air, he lowered his ears, flattening them against his skull. A low growl escaped him. His tail between his legs, he trotted up the steps, nose to the ground. He was nearing the boy's room. His tongue hung out of his mouth, but a moment later, he drew it back into his mouth. Now his fangs sank past his lips, overhanging his mouth. He bared his teeth, approaching the boy's bedroom door.

The Many Eyes of the Monster

MATT WANDERED THROUGH an odd neighborhood. It looked familiar, as though he'd been there before. But it also was somewhat different from any place he'd ever been. The nuances were hard to describe for one major reason. Several of the houses along this street were burnt or hollowed out. The damage appeared to be caused by bomb blasts. Somehow, he made his way through the rubble and around a fallen oak that stretched all the way across the road.

Urgent pulses flared through him. He headed for the nearest house untouched by the catastrophe. It was a brown house with a white porch railing and white window trim, which stood between a burnt home and one that had been gutted and knocked flat. He was on a mission, searching for something. What he was after remained a mystery. As he approached the brown house, a sign on the front door stood out. Glaring, red letters declared: GET OUT! YOU ARE HEREBY ORDERED TO VACATE THE PREMISES.

Matt stopped dead. His tongue tried to retreat down his throat. He clamped his jaws down hard, gritting his teeth. His tongue got the message and settled back into its rightful place. He rushed down the driveway toward the backyard. Nearing a fence gate, he noticed that there was suddenly snow on the ground. A huge pile of it towered in front of him. Out of nowhere, a man dressed in a white suit and matching loafers appeared and came out the back gate. He was an old fella with brilliant white hair and a matching mustache and beard. His eyes were soft and brown. He smiled at Matt as he walked past.

"The snow is my gift," he said. "Take as much as you need."

"For what?" Matt asked.

The man pointed across the street behind them. There Matt saw a blue house engulfed in flames. He was about to ask the guy what he was supposed to do, when the man handed him a shovel and commanded, "Go!"

Before he could protest, the man was gone. He threw the shovel down and ran back the way he'd come. He would have kept on going, too, if a familiar voice hadn't sounded behind him.

"Matt, Matt. Help me."

"Milo?" Matt's eyes widened.

That's when he realized Milo was trapped inside the burning house. He whipped around and booked back to where he'd dropped the shovel, wondering how to transport the snow to the house. As he came up the drive, he saw Randy, Bobby, and Jeff. They were standing in front of a red pick-up truck. All three of them had shovels. Already, a large pile of snow was in the truck bed. Matt grabbed his shovel from the ground and pitched in. When they had enough snow, they drove over to the house and shoveled it onto the fire. Somehow, it put the fire out and spared the house from serious damage. The right side of the house was blackened on the outside, though the structure remained standing.

Matt and the others hurried inside. Milo came out from under a desk, where he'd been cowering. He ran to Matt and hugged him. After Milo let go, Matt watched him retreat from the house. He was just about to leave when Jeff's sister Rachel appeared. She accosted him, jabbing at his chest with her finger. He backed up, but she kept coming, glaring.

"You can predict the future, but you can't talk to the dead," she snapped.

Matt sat bolt upright, slamming awake. Gasping, he rubbed his forehead with the back of his hand.

"Matt, Matt! Help."

Matt flinched, jerking back into the headboard. That sounded just like Milo, he thought. He looked around, trying to focus in the dark. Garrett was asleep on the floor, but otherwise, he was alone. Holding his breath, he listened for a moment but heard nothing further. Just then, Garrett whispered in his sleep. A shriek died on Matt's lips.

"Milo, where are you? Why can't I find you?" Gar moaned. He was on the verge of tears.

What's going on here, Matt wondered. He closed his eyes for a moment. God, please take care of Milo and guide him through whatever trouble is coming his way, he prayed.

His hackles were raised. He sniffed the carpet in front of the boy's room. Someone inside wasn't a tenant, but he was with the boy, so that was fine. It was the other presence that troubled him. He stood in front of the door and looked to his right. That direction was where the point of unauthorized entry had occurred. He lowered his muzzle to the carpet again. It appeared that the fiend had traveled this way. Lifting his head, Buster sniffed the air. He turned his back on the boy's room. The intruder's scent was oozing from the room a few feet up on the right. His ears rose at a sudden noise then flattened against his skull. He bent down, muscles tautening.

The door to the room of interest opened little by little. A shadowy figure emerged. It was a man, judging by the scent. Buster waited for the moment the intruder seemed most vulnerable and sprang at him. Growling, he leveled the man. He stepped onto the man's chest and pinned him, baring his teeth. His uttered a ferocious snarl. The frightened fiend wrestled him off. Buster snapped his jaws at the guy as he tried to get up, snatching his coat.

The man darted forward just enough to escape his grip. Buster bounded after him. He chased the man down the stairs, watching him exit through the front door. Whimpering and pacing, Buster scratched at the front door. His ears didn't lie: he could hear the intruder retreating. Based on the odor of fear the man was exuding, he wouldn't be coming back tonight. He panted, licked his paw, and raced upstairs. When he got to the boy's room, he scratched at the door and whined. His duty was fulfilled, and he wished to return home.

Matt uttered an unpleasant word when he heard scratching at his door. As it got louder, he heard a dog whine. It can't be, can it? He grabbed his baseball bat and shook Garrett awake.

"What now?" Gar muttered. Matt didn't have to answer. Garrett sat up when he heard the ruckus. "Somewhere out there is a being who believes that you and I should never need more than two hours of sleep," he grumbled.

"I think Buster's out there," Matt replied.

"What if it's the mysterious wolf or the pit bull?"

"Should that be the case, I've got a bat."

"Lend me your hockey stick."

Matt pointed at the closet. Gar retrieved the stick. "I've always wondered why you have this. I mean, you've never even played hockey."

"Focus, Gar."

They met at the door. Matt paused and looked at Garrett, who motioned him on. Garrett held the hockey stick aloft, poised to strike. Matt nodded and eased the door open. They leaned out to see Buster sitting in front of the door, his tail wagging at them.

"He looks harmless," Matt said, and they put the weapons aside. He patted Buster's head. "Good boy. Who's a good boy?"

Buster licked his hand.

"Okay, how'd he get in?" Garrett asked. He trembled, gulping as he remembered the open deck door from earlier.

"I dunno. We'd better take him home before Mr. Welker gets concerned, though."

"How are we gonna get him there? I don't exactly trust him not to run off," Garrett added.

Matt thought for a moment. "There's some rope in with my dad's tools. We'll tie that around him."

"We could always use the tow rope," Gar suggested.

"No. If Welker is in on it, I don't want him seeing that we found that stuff."

"True. But if Buster was warding off a threat to you earlier, then it would seem that Welker isn't in on it."

"Yeah, but like you said before, we should remain alert."

"I was right for once? Huzzah."

As they headed down the hall, Buster followed them.

Garrett laughed. "Maybe I was wrong to distrust him."

Matt recoiled, for he glanced down as Gar spoke and darned if Buster didn't cast a reproachful look at Garrett. "I'm not taking any chances," he said at last. He retrieved the rope and leashed Buster up.

Garrett followed them out the door. Buster wagged his tail when they got outside, ears perking up. His tongue dangled out the side of his mouth. Matt trotted across the drive to Mr. Welker's porch and knocked on the door. There was no response. Garrett reached past him and pressed the doorbell. Buster barked twice in response to hearing the noise. A few moments later, Lawrence Welker opened the door, hair mussed up. His bleary eyes beheld the two boys and his dog.

"What's going on? What are you doing with my dog?" he asked through yawns.

"Uh, we found him in my front yard," Matt lied. He didn't know how Buster had gotten in the house, and he didn't feel like bewildering Mr. Welker further.

"This is beginning to get on my nerves. For the life of me, I can't figure out how he keeps getting out. Get in here, you crazy mutt," he demanded. Buster skulked up to him, and he removed the rope from the dog's neck and handed it back to Matt. "Thanks for bringing him home."

"You're welcome. Have a good night, Mr. Welker."

"Yeah, what's left of it. You too," he added.

After they returned to the house, Garrett saw that Matt was shaking. "Hey, it's gonna be okay."

"Why was Buster here, and how'd he get in?" Matt queried.

Bracing himself for Matt's ire, he replied, "I don't know why, but I might know how. Perhaps he was somehow brought in through the deck door upstairs."

Matt frowned at him. "Why on earth would you think that?"

Sighing, he explained, "Because when I went up to get your dad's robe, the door was open just a crack."

"What? I locked the deadbolt last Sunday, and I checked it Friday night. It was locked then."

"I don't know. I think if I just had a glass of Kool-Aid, it'd help me think," he answered, attempting to slink away.

Matt exploded. "Don't you walk off. Why didn't you tell me this earlier?"

"It didn't seem like a big deal. I figured we were safe, since the spirit soldier told us to come here."

"You should have let me know, so we could've searched the house," he grumbled.

"I didn't feel it was necessary."

"Ugh. Unbelievable." Matt threw his hands up.

"I'm sorry. I just didn't want to worry you over what could easily be nothing."

"Forget it. You go get your Kool-Aid. I've got things to do."

"What do you mean? Where're you going?" Garrett asked.

Matt refused to reply. Garrett tailed him upstairs. Matt grabbed his trusty knife and his Louisville Slugger. He also pocketed the night vision scope.

"Matt, now is not a good time to go postal."

Ignoring this statement, Matt sidestepped him and scowled. Garrett swallowed hard. He knew that expression all too well. *No doubt he's about do something gutsy and foolish*, he realized.

"What are you gonna do?"

"I'm going to investigate that bed and breakfast. You are free to do whatever. I would say you should probably go back to sleep. You seem to be very tired," Matt retorted.

Garrett eyed him with a stubborn glare. "Tired? Are you bloody serious? If you're going, count me in."

"You sure?"

"I can tell when there's no talking you out of something. Stop doubting me. I'm not about to let you go alone. Besides, one would assume that you can also tell when there's no way to talk me out of something."

"Fine by me." Matt smirked.

Crossing his arms over his chest, Gar added, "We really shouldn't leave until you're done being angry at me."

Matt gawked at him and rolled his eyes. "Whatever. I'm over being mad. Now let's go."

"Hooray for middle of the night quests." As they left, he whispered, "Matt, we're not going inside the B&B, are we? Because trespassing on private property is one thing, but breaking and entering is another thing entirely."

"I don't know yet," he admitted.

"I'm just saying, if we're gonna do a B&E, why not find out what's in Welker's basement while we're at it," he joked.

"Because Buster would eat you," Matt returned.

"Can I just say one thing? Do we really want to risk getting arrested? For what?"

"Do we really want to risk not having vital information that we may be able to use to take these wackos down?"

Garrett sighed. "And if we find nothing?"

"Then at least we tried to do something. But we need a one-up on our enemy. Besides, I don't think we'd have been warned to stay away if there was nothing there. Wouldn't you agree?"

"I guess," he said.

"Here, take the bat. I've got my knife."

"Thanks." Trudging down the road, Garrett flashed back to his imaginary movie about the '30s and the guy with the pinstripe suit and fedora. "Man, I sure wish I had a Chicago piano right about now."

"A what? Oh right, a tommy gun. Where'd that come from?"

"Never mind. Random thought."

Matt managed a smile, and they continued in silence. When they neared their destination, he said, "All right, the B&B is a couple of blocks up. We should approach from behind."

"Yeah," Garrett agreed, "let's head to Locust Street and enter the alley that runs parallel to Richard Street."

"Does that alley go through?"

"Yes. It goes on for about a block before it ends. It runs right behind the B&B."

"I didn't know that."

"Of course you didn't. You can't see it from the front of the house because of the fence."

"Right."

A block up, they turned onto Locust Street. Halfway down the block, they went into the alley and slipped through the shadows, praying that no one saw or heard them. As they approached the high board fence, the sound of voices forced them to cringe back. The glare of headlights cast light between the cracks of the boards. Grateful that the fence had no opening in the rear, they held their breath as an engine roared to life. Step by step, they encroached upon the fence once more. The voices seemed to get nearer, stopping them in their tracks again.

"I'm telling you, I went to brief him, and D'Amato ran off like a scolded dog. I didn't have time to ask him what was up. He ran right past the van, didn't even take notice of me. Even ran past his own truck, the numbskull. The boss should've had me go," a stern male voice said.

"All I know is, Morriston's gonna be very upset if Sori finds out about all these setbacks," another man replied.

"Hey, when's Capone due, already? I'm starving," the first guy grumbled.

"Capone's shift begins in half an hour," his cohort informed him.

The first guy groaned. "Ya think D'Amato'll show up with ole Scarface when he gets here?"

"Nah. That incompetent jerk took off after the incident, didn't he? And I still haven't heard from him yet. Capone checked in a moment ago, and he hasn't heard from him either. But if one Chester A. D'Amato doesn't get his keister back here soon, the boss'll rip him a new one. It'll be even worse for him if Sori gets wind of it. I wonder where he could be."

"He prolly went back to his truck to get some shut eye. Come on, let's knock off early, get some breakfast."

"Fine. Get in the van."

"Personally, I don't get why the boss is so afraid of a couple of runts. The twerps can't even vote."

"Yet is the key word. Anyway, your job is not to ask questions. Your job is to do as you're told. Is that clear, Raphael?" snapped the second guy. Apparently, he was higher in rank than Raphael.

"Whatever you say, lord Eddie," Raphael muttered.

Matt waited until they heard the van drive off then motioned for Garrett to head back down the alley. *I wasn't thinking. We'd never have gotten over that fence*, Garrett realized, shaking his head.

When they got back to Locust Street, Matt whispered, "We should use the front door. It's already broken, so we'll be able to get in faster."

Garrett nodded. They walked up to Richard Street and followed it to the front of the house. After a quick glance around, they headed to the porch. Garrett's eyes landed on the dilapidated door. His spine tingled. Again, he flashed back to his movie. He saw the speakeasy and the mafia man with the yellow daisy on his lapel. The sign above the entrance warned that those who entered were beyond rescue. For a moment, the image was so real that he could touch it. He almost wandered right into it, but all this faded, and now the street sign that read REALM OF MONSTERS flashed through his mind. He drew in a ragged breath.

Matt took no notice of this. Climbing the canted steps, he was struck by an eerie sense of serendipity. It's amnesia. The task is to discover who you are and what your mission is. Then you have to go about carrying it out, he remembered. He flinched, stopping in mid-stride. Garrett collided with him. Matt toppled forward. Gar grabbed his collar and hauled him up.

"Sorry about that," Gar whispered.

"My fault," he muttered.

He yanked so hard on the broken screen door that it sprang off its hinge. He tried to grab it, but he was too slow. Again, Garrett came through, this time by obstructing its path. The door whacked him on the head. He bit his tongue as he lifted the door by its sides, pulling it away from his face, and set the offending screen door on the porch floor.

"You're lucky that door wasn't super heavy. I'm gonna end up with a concussion because of your clumsiness one of these days," he muttered.

"Sorry."

Matt reached through the diamond shaped hole and unlocked the door. He opened the heavy door with increased caution and managed not to break it. They rushed into a large foyer and shut the door. A staircase loomed before them. It was coated with dirt and dust, but even with the grime, it was obvious that this had once been a grand piece of woodwork. Although he couldn't be sure, given the lack of lighting, Matt suspected the staircase was made from oak, like the door. The railings were curved at the ends and had thin, decorative posts with rectangular ends and long, spindle-like balusters. Aside from three inches on either side of the steps, the stairs were covered with a musty carpet runner.

Taking this in, they at first dismissed the spectral quiet that surrounded them. That is, until a dull clinking sound invaded the silence.

"What is that?" Matt whispered as the sound grew crisper and louder.

Garrett gaped and pointed at the stairs. Rolling down the steps were several quarters, pennies, and nickels.

"Huh. Guess this place really is haunted," Matt remarked.

Garrett gawked at him. "That's all you've got to say?"

"I don't have it in me to be bothered with this."

"Just who is the master of this house?" Garrett inquired.

"Let's go," Matt said.

As the coins collected at the bottom of the stairs, Gar asked, "Where to first?"

"Let's check the upstairs first."

"Are you nuts? How are we gonna escape if those goons come back? Plus, what if someone's here and hears us moving around up there?"

"No one's here. That Capone guy isn't due to arrive for about half an hour. These people must work in shifts. We'll have to be quick about it."

"Okay, two things. One, what if those guys were lying? Two, I'd rather check the basement first."

"We can't stand here arguing. We'll go up first and work our way back down. That way, when we're done, we'll be down here and can get out quicker."

"When you put it that way, the plan totally works for me."

They zoomed up the steps. The upstairs was huge. Total, there were nine doors to check along the hallway. It didn't take as long as they figured to work their way down, however. The rooms were big, but since they were unfurnished, they were able to open the door, sweep it with the scope, and move on. All in all, it took just minutes to get to the last door, which turned out to be the entrance to the attic.

"Let's get this over with," Gar moaned. "I hate attics in haunted houses."

Matt shivered and nodded. They trudged up the narrow stairway. When they got to the top and stepped into the attic, they heard something crunch underfoot. Immediately, they glanced down.

"No. So much no-ness," Garrett rasped.

The floor was littered with dead ants, flies, and spiders. Matt did his best to hold in a shriek. It came out as a gurgling sound. He used the scope to look around. The entire attic contained nothing but dead bugs. He handed the night vision scope to Gar. As he gazed around the attic floor, Garrett had a word blaring over and over through his mind. Devastation, he thought. Following this, an image came, called forth by the word. It was from one of the video game mods he'd played. He saw himself standing on a battlefield with thousands of demons coming at him. In his hands was a chain gun, and he depressed the trigger mightily as rage and fear coursed through him. Matt's voice brought him back to reality.

"The attic's clear. Let's head down."

Garrett stepped aside, allowing Matt to go ahead of him. As he followed, the strangest thing happened. He was staring at the back of Matt's head, when a bald eagle appeared—translucent and superimposed over Matt like a movie special effect. The eagle had its back to him and was flying forward. He swore that it was screeching. At the bottom of the stairs, the eagle soared off ahead of them. I did not just see that, did I, he wondered.

Matt turned to shut the door behind them, and his body went numb. All the warmth inside him fled. Standing in front of Garrett was a huge lion. He heard it growl as it leapt past him. It turned translucent as it fled down the hall. Matt took off, bolting for the stairs. Though he was afraid of the beast, he just had to get another look at it. Garrett shot after him, forgetting to close the attic door.

"Matt, wait. What happened?" he shouted.

Matt didn't reply. When they reached the staircase, Garrett saw the eagle again, swooping down from above Matt's head. He watched it glide with ease to a perch on top of a lion's head. Oh no, he thought. Both animals faded before his eyes. Great, we've stumbled onto a ghost zoo.

At the bottom of the stairs, Matt turned to him, noting that Gar was very pale. "Let's just go on to the basement. I doubt there's anything in these other rooms."

"Agreed. I think we have ten minutes or so before certain doom. Which way?"

Matt shrugged and went right, hoping they were headed in the right direction. The first door they came to opened on what seemed to have been a library. Vacant shelves lined the walls. Here and there, a few freestanding bookcases had fallen over onto their sides. The rest of the room was bare. They pressed on until they found the kitchen. Inside, they noticed an old woodstove and a porcelain sink on a cracked, marble base and two doors. One was a pantry, and the other led to the basement. Taking the steps two at a time, they sped down and poked around. At first, it seemed that the basement was just as abandoned as the rest of the house. There were two sections, an open main room with no furniture and a furnace room. For such a huge place, this basement sure is small, Matt noted.

"There's nothing here," Garrett remarked.

"Hold on. Is it me, or does this basement seem smaller than it should for a place this size?"

Blinking, Gar said, "Hey, you're right. Look there."

He was pointing at the wall that faced the stairway. Matt gawked. "There's a door handle there. How'd we miss this?"

"Well, the door is the same color as the wall, so it blends in."

Matt yanked the door open. It swung outward, revealing an old workshop. There were tool benches and worktables all throughout the room. Against the wall to their right, a huge desk full of computer processors spanned the whole side of the room. Above the processors, fixed to the wall in some kind of casing, were several glass screens, similar to the old analog TV screens. Matt estimated that there were at least twenty of them.

"What is this?" he said.

Spotting a label that was stuck to the top of one of the monitors, Garrett read, "Test block one A. What does that mean?"

Matt gasped. "Gar, look."

Garrett peered at the monitors. He saw that each monitor had a camera feed displaying different rooms. They were all uniquely furnished and appeared to be from different houses. Some rooms were unoccupied, others had people in them. Most of the monitors looked in on people who were asleep in their beds, but not all of the rooms were bedrooms. A few were kitchens or living rooms with men and women talking or watching TV. In one of the kitchens, a couple sat around the table, chatting with one another. No sound came from the speakers that were on the desk next to the processors.

"What's going on? Are these people aware that they're being watched?"

"I don't think so, Mattie."

Scowling, he said, "I don't like vandalism, but still. Hand me the bat."

"What are you doing?" Garrett asked as he complied.

"I'm gonna break these monitors."

"Matt, that's wrong."

"So's spying on people."

"Two wrongs don't make a right."

"I know. But I'm not perfect, and neither are you."

"What does that mean?"

"It means—" Crash. He hit one of the screens with the bat and bashed in the processor below it.

"That was a terrible justification. You probably just cost the taxpayers thousands."

"No, these buffoons did. Do you think the American people would willingly fund this?"

"No, but then again, there is the Patriot Act."

"That was sold to the people as a way to protect them, not intrude on their rights. But you're right: America tolerated a huge power grab. That shouldn't have been allowed, but it doesn't give these creeps the right to do this. This is wrong."

Garrett was about to protest again, when something on one of the screens caught his eye. The color drained from his face. He gripped Matt's shoulder.

"What's up?"

"I recognize this room. Look, it's Liz's. That's her sleeping right there."

Matt squinted at the screen. "Oh, man. This is a new low, even for the government."

Gar's face turned red. He balled his hands into fists. Unclenching his fists, he said, "Gimme that bat. This one's mine."

"You sure?" Matt asked, handing him the bat.

"I got this."

Garrett smashed the glass screen to smithereens. He hit it so hard the bat bounced off the screen and ricocheted right back at his face. He dodged it and was lucky to avoid rocketing pieces of glass as well. As Matt watched, the face of the lion from earlier appeared, superimposed over Garrett's face. Although he was sure Gar didn't hear it, a loud roar echoed through Matt's ears. The deeper part of him spoke up again.

"The flame of justice burns in him," it observed. Matt flinched.

Garrett took the liberty of breaking the rest of the monitors then worked on obliterating the processors.

When he finished, he said, "You realize this isn't going to stop them."

"We've done what we can. For now," Matt added.

Garrett didn't like what he was implying. "You mean this isn't over?"

"I don't think so," Matt answered.

"What else is there to do," he groaned.

"I don't know," Matt repeated.

"Can we get out of here now?"

"We may."

"Touche."

They raced up the stairs and back to the front of the house. As they neared the door, they spotted headlights in the driveway through the gaps in the boarded up windows. Matt pulled Garrett out of the window's sightline. Even though it was covered, he wasn't taking the chance that the headlights would expose their presence. They waited with bated breath until the vehicle passed to the side of the house.

"He's parking out back like the others. Quick, out the door," Matt said.

They eased it open, grateful the driver hadn't noticed the missing screen door. Outside, they shot off the porch. When they got to the end of the sidewalk, Matt veered left and flew up Richard Street in a blind panic. Garrett dashed after him. When he caught up, he grabbed Matt by the arm and dragged him across the street. At the next block, he led them along the side street, bearing right, and then two blocks over. There, they crossed the street.

Matt followed him north up Wasson Street. He had assumed that their flight was random, but it soon became clear that they were taking a roundabout way to Garrett's. Just before the next intersection, Gar pointed to a bush in someone's yard. Panting, he motioned for Matt to duck behind the bush. They hit their knees. Matt stared at him.

"This is my cousin's house, so it's okay," Garrett explained between breaths.

"Ah," he grunted. "Why are we going to your house? I thought it wasn't safe."

"Matt, if they assume it was us that did the damage, where's the first place they'll look? Your house. Besides, I wanna check on something."

"What?"

He shook his head. "I don't know yet. Just got a funny feeling, ya know?"

Matt nodded. "All right. Let's go."

As they crept through the night, gripping their weapons tight in their fists, the wind picked up, bringing the scent of burned leaves with it. *I don't care about the Halloween-like atmosphere anymore. I've had enough scares to last a lifetime,* Garrett thought.

The Mysterious Milo

AT LONG LAST, they reached Garrett's, approaching from the alley. Garrett eased the latch on the gate up, and they slipped into the yard. He started toward the garage.

"Aren't you going to close the gate?" Matt whispered.

"No. In case we need to make a quick exit."

Matt frowned and followed him to the garage. Facing the yard was a side door with a window. Garrett peered inside but could see nothing.

"Hand me the scope, Matt."

Matt placed the scope in his hand. Garrett put it up to his eye. He could see two cars inside. One was his mother's car. He knew because he recognized the cross air freshener hanging from her rearview mirror. That was fine. When they had left yesterday, they had taken his father's car. He wasn't able to determine whether or not the car adjacent to his mother's was Dad's. He frowned. It figured that the license plate of the adjacent car wasn't visible from this angle. He reached into his pocket to grab his keys and found it empty. His other hand dipped into the remaining pants pocket. Nothing there either.

"Crap. I left my keys at your house," Garrett muttered.

"Should we go and get them?" Matt asked.

"Nah. Come on, we'll just snoop around the property."

He followed Garrett as he peered in the windows at the back of the house. "What are you looking for, anyway?"

Gar shrugged. "Lights on, signs of life."

Matt groaned.

"Keep it down," he whispered.

Matt rolled his eyes, and they continued around the side of the house. There was nothing of note until they came to the window outside Garrett's room. No light shined from the window. However, as they approached the glass, Garrett jumped back. Matt moved away from the window's sightline, falling in line behind him. Gar pressed himself against the siding.

"What is it?" Matt murmured.

"Sh."

Garrett eased forward just enough to see into the window. He crouched, prepared to duck if need be. In his room, a man was sitting at the desk, using the computer. Though the darkness made it impossible to tell, Gar suspected that this man was not his father. Curiosity got the better of him, and he ducked down and crept forward. Matt followed, also ducking. When they got around to the front of the house, they stood up. There were no lights on in the rest of the house, and when they looked in the windows, no one else was present. Garrett trotted to the back door and turned the knob. It was locked.

"Now what?" Matt said.

"Let's get out of here," he croaked.

They burst through the open gate. Garrett latched it behind them. It was another hour before they reached Matt's, due to the meandering path they forged. Although it seemed no one had followed and they hadn't encountered anything suspicious, their hearts beat like mad when they entered the house.

Milo sat up on the floor, jerking away from the pillow. He tossed the sleeping bag aside and got up, unsure what had awakened him.

A sense of urgency stole over him, and he knew he needed to leave the room. First, however, he hurried to the window. He paused and looked it over. No good, he thought, it's got a screen. Leaving the window, he crept to the door, so as not to wake Jason. There was no time to explain.

He left the door open behind him and trotted down the hall. He intended to go up to the second floor. On his way to the staircase, he stopped just once. As he passed the front door, he had the urge to halt. He examined the door for a moment then unlocked it and pulled it open, exposing the screen door. Immediately, he shot up the staircase to the second floor and made his way to the attic door. Jason had never showed him where the attic entrance was located. Still, he knew where he was going even as he stepped through the doorway.

Although loathe to go on without a light, he shut the door without a sound and sidled up the steps. He slipped lithely over the floorboards and ducked behind the chimney. There was nowhere else to hide. He pressed against the back of the chimney, barely breathing. A grimace donned his face as he noticed how free of clutter it was up here. He'd been in his own attic last year to help Garrett bring down the Christmas decorations. It was a total mess by comparison but offered hiding spots.

Minutes later, his heart leapt into his throat as the attic door creaked open. Uh-oh, he thought. The steps squeaked as someone came up. He had no idea who this person was or why he was being chased. When his pursuer got to the top of the stairs, there was a brief pause. Soft thuds issued from the boards as the person stepped forward, drawing closer and closer to his quarry. Milo held his breath, heart hammering in protest. Just before his stalker got to the chimney, he found himself sinking through the floor. He felt no pain, and he hadn't broken through the boards. He simply slid through them. He saw the floor as he passed through, watching his legs descend into the hallway below.

All of a sudden, he was standing in the middle of the second floor hall. Above him, he could hear subtle noises, as though the house was settling. But he knew better. He ran to the stairwell. As he stepped on the first stair, the stairway vanished, and he found himself standing on a basement landing. He raced down the steps and took refuge under a pool table, grabbing a pool cue off the table just before he crawled under. He had no idea how long he cowered there. Milo's eyelids drooped. His eyes began to close when he noticed legs standing in front of the pool table. His eyelids shot up. Boots were in front of him. He shrank away, positioning the pool cue in front of him like a jousting stick. Holding his breath, he waited.

"Milo," a warm male voice said, "it's okay to come out now."

Milo stiffened, unconvinced. Yet moment by moment, the tension faded, and at last, he felt at peace. He lowered the pool cue.

"Come out. You can go back to Jason's room and sleep. The diversion worked."

Milo scrambled out from under the table and saw a man in a soldier's uniform before him. The man knelt down, grasping Milo in his arms. A gentle smile was on his lips, and his eyes were resplendent with love.

"Who are you?" Milo asked, tears of relief streaming down his face.

"All you need to know is that I'm a guardian. I will watch over you while you sleep."

"And protect me from the bad guy?" he added.

"Yes. Let's go back upstairs."

Milo hesitated, still locked in the soldier's embrace. "Is Garrett all right?" he inquired suddenly.

"He is. He may be in some danger now, though. He has done a brave and foolish thing, and even more enemies have been made. But I will help as much as I can. Don't worry."

Although he frowned, Milo whispered, "Okay."

He followed the man back to Jason's room. When he lay snug in his sleeping bag, the man turned away and walked toward the door.

"Where are you going?" Milo said.

"I must keep a close watch outside to make sure he doesn't come back," the soldier explained as he walked out the door, closing it behind him.

"What do you think that guy was doing at your house?" Matt asked.

"How should I know?" he snapped.

"And why was he on your computer?"

"Probably checking to see what sites I visit." Gar shrugged.

"Or planting something on your computer."

"Maybe. But couldn't he just do that by hacking?"

"I guess."

Garrett's mind was elsewhere as Matt rambled on, "Do you suppose this could have something to do with that package your dad got?"

"Wait, what?"

"The package your dad made you wait for yesterday. Hello? Do you think that guy being at your house has something to do with that package?"

"Maybe," Garrett replied.

His nonchalance got on Matt's nerves. "What is up, man?"

"I'm trying to figure out if I should tell Liz that some government goons have been spying on her." Gar ran his hands through his hair.

Matt's frustration evaporated. "I don't know if you want to upset her like that."

"Well, she does have a right to know."

"Is it worth making her paranoid? And what if she doesn't believe you?"

"There exists the possibility that she'll think I'm wacko-bonkers, but then, if she doesn't think so already, I doubt this'll be the incident that forces her to that conclusion. As for upsetting her, I don't want to, but Liz can't stand anyone being too protective of her. If she ever did find out about this and that I hadn't told her, she'd fry my bones and chew 'em up like bacon."

"Guess you better tell her."

"Guess so."

"Let's hit the hay," Matt suggested, yawning.

"I'm all for that," Garrett agreed.

When they got up to his room, he fell asleep as soon as his head hit the pillow. Garrett remained awake. Tears settled on his cheeks as he thought of what Liz had endured without knowing it. They can't be allowed to do such things, he decided, a glower darkening his face. Rage rose within, and he almost roared aloud. For a moment, he wished that he had Buster's canines and could insert them into the creeps who had watched her. Liz, he thought, heart beating like mad, I live to make you laugh, to brighten your days as you do mine. Will you break if I tell you? He hoped not. She'd always been strong, and if she broke, then he would crack apart as well. As long as he'd known her, he'd tried to emulate her courage and joy. She had the freest spirit he had ever seen, tempered by a self-sacrificing will. He sighed. Don't worry, precious. We'll get through this mess.

At ten in the morning, he got up, uncertain if he'd slept at all. Matt was still out. Gar beamed. Aw, he looks like a little kid all tuckered out from play. I'm tempted to ruffle his hair. Instead, he grabbed his phone, leaving the room, and dialed Liz's number. She answered on the third ring, sounding tired.

"Hello."

"Morning, precious."

"Garrett? Why are you calling so early?"

"Maybe I just wanted to hear your voice."

"Uh-huh. I don't buy it. What's going on?"

"Look, do you have some free time?"

"Yeah. Dad's here today, so I can go out."

"Meet me at Matt's. I need to talk to you."

Alarmed by his tone, she said, "What about?"

"I'll tell you when you get here. How soon can I expect you?"

"About an hour."

"All right. Bye."

"Bye."

"Oh, and Liz?"

"Yeah?"

"You still have that pepper spray?"

"Yeah."

"Bring it with you."

"Why?"

"Just in case."

"What do you mean just in case? What's going on?"

"I'll tell you in person."

"Fine."

"Don't forget: pepper spray."

"Got it. I always carry it in my purse anyway."

"Good. I love you."

"I love you, too."

When she arrived, Garrett was pacing on the porch. He's wound up tighter than a rubber band. This can't be good, she realized. Hoping to evoke a smile, she quipped, "You'd better not even think of breaking up with me. I'm the best option life's gonna hand you."

He frowned instead of smiling, which sent goosebumps down her arms.

"Get up here. Did you carry your pepper spray?"

"Why? You and Matt planning to use it for some nefarious teenage boy experiment? 'Cause I wouldn't advise snorting it." When his eyes grew misty rather than amused, she halted. "What's up, Gar? I don't like this."

He wrapped his arms around her and held her. When she drew back, he said, "You'd better come inside."

She followed without a word, noting that he locked the door behind them. Holding her hand, he led her to the kitchen.

"You're gonna want to sit down for this," he said.

"Where's Matt?" she asked.

"Sleeping."

"Isn't he usually up by now?"

"We had a rough night," he explained.

"Gamers," she muttered, feigning annoyance. This also failed to draw a smile from him. "So why am I here? Miss me that much?"

He kissed her fiercely. "Always," he murmured, choking up.

He half-expected her to tease him about this desperate display of affection, but she said, "Tell me what's wrong."

"I don't want to freak you out."

"Too late for that," she remarked.

"I don't even know where to start," he admitted.

"Start with the worst part first, so we can get it over with, and if there's more, backtrack after that."

"Okay. This is gonna sound totally nuts, but here it is: last night, Matt and I discovered that some government goons—at least, we think they're government goons, because they're connected to our congressman. Anyway, they had all these computers and these monitors showing different rooms. They were spying on people, and it was clear they had a live camera feed. And then I noticed your room on one of the monitors. You were sleeping."

"What?" she interrupted. *Am I in the Twilight Zone or something,* she wondered, shuddering. Her eyes grew large. *I'm never gonna feel at ease taking a shower ever again. What if the pervs have been taping me in there? Oh my word.* Inhaling slowly, she forced her mind to go blank. *Do not give in to this,* she told herself.

"Yeah. And so Matt and I bashed the monitors and computers to bits and fled."

Blinking, she said, "Wait. How—and where—did you uncover all this?"

"In the basement of that old Richard Street Bed and Breakfast."

She narrowed her eyes. "You broke into that abandoned B&B? What were you doing there?"

"Ah, well, here's where it gets dicey. Let me explain the events of the last nine days." He explained about Norm Morriston, Buster, and everything else, with the exception of his visions.

When he finished, she yelled, "Are you mad? How could you put yourself in danger like that? And Matt, too. You two should have your heads examined."

"We bloody well had to do something," he protested.

"I commend you for your heroism. But don't put yourself at risk," she pleaded.

"I'm glad I did. If we hadn't, we wouldn't know those bloody cretins were spying on you. And we wouldn't have stopped them."

"That's beside the point. Let the perverts spy on me. It won't do them any good," she retorted. She put her hands on the sides of his face. "But I don't want to lose you. Do you understand?" she whispered.

He nodded.

"Someday, I want to have a family with you and a life all our own. So don't take stupid risks like that. You have no idea what kind of people you're messing with. It's not a game, Garrett. You can't just die and start over. There are no cheat codes for this kind of thing. Tell me this is the end of it," she begged.

Clasping her hands, he said, "I will do what I can to avoid danger, but we may have to take them on again. I just don't know."

I depend on you, she thought but could not say. You think I'm so strong, but it's this secret dream which keeps me going. She sighed. His mind was made up, but so was hers. I always knew he had a hero hidden inside. You can't hinder someone like that, she decided. You've got to let them be and, if possible, nurture that kind of courage. "I understand," she told him.

"You do?"

"Yes. But I still want kids someday."

With a killer smile, he replied, "And I shall do my best to provide them for you."

"Save it for when we're married, Romeo," she warned. Her eyes filled with delight.

"Deal," he said.

"There is one more thing," Liz added.

"Dandy. And what might that be?"

"I need to be by your side."

"What? No way. That's out of the question."

She cast an admonishing stare at him. He sighed, relenting. "I can see that your will is ironclad. I guess I have no choice."

She grinned, and he noted her deep satisfaction. He couldn't resist smiling back. "You sure are cute when you're determined," he observed.

"Thank you. You're kinda creepy looking when you're stubborn, though," she taunted.

"Nice. Wound me right through the heart. I see how you are."

"Aw, come here," she said and kissed his forehead. "I take it back. You're as adorable as a Rottweiler Poodle mix."

He burst out laughing. "How do you come up with this stuff?"

"I have my muse," she responded with an adoring gaze.

"I am pretty inspiring, aren't I?"

"Yeah. So what are we gonna do now, huh, goofball?" She tousled his hair.

"We could wake up Matt, or we could play Mortal Kombat."

"I'm all for Mortal Kombat."

"Really? The Madden girl likes combat games?"

"Are you serious? I play Gears of War and Call of Duty all the time. And I used to annihilate Randy at MK4."

"Ho-ho. I can see I'm getting called out."

"No, you're about to get whupped by a professional."

"Well played."

"You know it," she declared.

I am a lucky guy, he mused, although I am quite dreading our marital spats.

At two o'clock, Milo, who was playing tag with Jason on his front lawn, saw his parents pull up. He grabbed his backpack and raced to the car, waving goodbye to Jason.

"Momma, Daddy," he cried.

"Hey, buddy. Get in," his father said.

"Did you have fun, sweetie?" his mom asked.

"Uh-huh. Mom, Jason has a fort in his backyard. We were gonna sleep out there, but it was too scary."

"Aw. Well, maybe when you boys get a little older."

"Yeah."

As they pulled away, Milo noticed that neither of his parents spoke to each other. Any other time, soft laughs, conversation, and smiles aplenty were exchanged between them, but today they seemed distracted. He didn't like this one bit. Something's up, he thought. His body started shaking. Why couldn't everyone just tell the truth and be happy? Why all this pretending? He swallowed hard. When they got home, his parents went to the package on the table. It held their attention, though neither of them opened it.

"Dad, can I go play in my room?"

"What? Oh, sure. But don't be too loud, okay?"

"Okay."

He patted his son's head. Milo hurried to his room and shut the door, then slunk down to Garrett's room. The door, which Gar always kept closed, was ajar. He gulped and shoved it all the way open. The room was empty and looked as he'd last seen it, but something was off. There was a faint aroma, very much like cologne. Garrett wore cologne, but this stuff was nothing like what he wore. It smelled spicy and somehow brutish. He shuddered, leaning against the doorframe. He didn't want to enter the room, and he jerked back at the realization. That wasn't like him. Oh no, I'm being like everyone else, all different and stuff, he thought.

Frowning, he bolted into the room and pushed the door closed behind him. He was typically overjoyed at the chance to snoop through Garrett's stuff. Today, however, he ignored that impulse and gazed about the room for signs that someone else had been there. The only thing that caught his eye was a rumpled piece of paper on the desk next to the computer. Milo pulled the computer chair out just enough to sit in. He glanced at the piece of paper. There was nothing written on it, but it was ruffled and marred, as if someone had rested their arm on it, or it had been shifted around a bit. He turned on the computer.

He had never done anything on a computer other than play games when Garrett allowed it. But when it booted up, he clicked on the Internet Explorer browser. He could not read the names of the things he clicked on, and his eyes went blank as he used the mouse, clicking on the Tools icon on the taskbar. He set the mouse cursor on Internet Options. When the menu came up, he hit the Security tab. The security had been moved to its lowest setting. He reset it to medium-high and clicked the Privacy tab. That had also been set at the minimum. He reset this to medium-high as well.

Once he finished this, he went to the history and cleared it. Next, he checked the box that indicated it would delete the browsing history on exit. He had no clue what any of this stuff did, but he felt the imperativeness of his actions. Before he shut down the computer, his eyes landed on the taskbar and narrowed. There was an icon here that he didn't recognize, but it unnerved him. He put the cursor over it and could not read the description, because all he understood was "is." But whatever that word referred to, he knew it was something awful. He opened a desk drawer, grabbed a pen, and wrote down the letters of the program on the blank piece of paper. Then he went to the Start menu and hit Control Panel. He selected the Uninstall option and scrolled through the list until he found a program matching the letters of the one he'd written down. He highlighted it and hit Uninstall/Change.

He followed the directions by intuition as his blank eyes watched his hand on the mouse, then moved back to the screen. At last, the bad program was removed. He clicked on the Recycle Bin icon when he got back to the desktop screen. There was only one other item in the bin. It was a Word document named something "Find." Milo shivered as he emptied the bin.

Exiting out of the Recycle Bin, he was about to shut down the computer, when someone said, "Well done, Milo. I'll take it from here."

Standing over him was the soldier from the night before. "What's your name? How do you keep showing up?" Milo demanded.

"No time. I've got to delete the shadow copies."

"Shadow copies?" repeated Milo.

Ignoring him, the soldier placed his hand on the mouse and moved it all about. Milo lost track of what he was doing, something about restore points and extra copies. The man also muttered something about "scrubbing the drive," but Milo didn't get what he meant. When the man was finished, he let Milo turn off the computer. As they pulled away from the desk, the man stopped him.

"Grab Garrett's microphone for me, will you?"

"But I'm not supposed to touch that. I'd be dead if he found out."

"He'll have bigger problems if you don't."

Milo gasped and retrieved the mic. He handed it to the man.

"I need a knife. Do you know if Garrett has a pocketknife?"

Milo nodded. "He keeps it in his top dresser drawer so I can't get it."

The man searched the drawer. "Ah, here it is. Okay, now when I pry this casing open, I'll need you to do something for me."

"Um, okay."

The man slid the knife blade between the sides of the casing and pried it apart. He peered inside. Milo watched him stick the knife blade in. He appeared to cut something, his hand moving back and forth in a sawing motion.

"Okay, Milo, hold out your hand."

Milo opened his palm.

"When I dump this into your hand, don't drop it."

Milo nodded. The soldier shook the open casing above Milo's hand. Milo watched as a tiny, square object landed in his palm. It was smaller than a postage stamp and very thin. He closed his fingers around the object.

"Put that in your pocket."

Milo deposited the object into the pocket of his hoodie. Meanwhile, the man fixed the casing of the microphone. It looked as if it had never been touched. Milo sighed with relief.

"Put this back and come over to the bookcase," the man told him.

Milo did as he was told and joined the soldier at Garrett's game shelves. The soldier rummaged through the top shelf, which was high above Milo's head. At last, he curled his fingers around an object and brought his hand down. He placed the object in Milo's hand.

"This little thing is a spy camera. I need you to take this and the thing in your pocket out to the garage and use the hand sledge to break them. You got it?"

"Okay." Milo stuck the camera in his pocket beside the square thing.

"Be very careful. You don't want to let your parents catch you."

Milo flinched. "Why? Are they bad too?"

"No. But they'd get curious about what you're up to and stop you," the soldier explained.

"Got it."

Milo closed the door behind him. In the kitchen, he snatched his mom's keys off the hook by the back door. Man, he hoped they didn't check on him while he was gone. He'd really be in trouble then. *I'll just have to be real fast,* he thought, sneaking out to the garage. He opened the side door with the key. Breathing a sigh of relief, he entered the garage and closed the door behind him. The hand sledge was hanging on a pegboard toward the back of the garage.

He grabbed it, setting the camera and the square object on the worktable. He hefted up the little sledge and slammed it down on the square thing. It broke easy enough, requiring only three blows. But when he moved on to the camera, things got more difficult. It didn't break in three blows or even four. He kept hitting it, panting. His arm felt like it was gonna fall off. Still, the camera was intact. Cracked, but intact. He scowled. *Maybe I'm not strong enough,* he thought, though he decided on one more try. This time, he used both hands and hoisted the sledge above his head. He brought it down hard, giving it all he had. *Bam.* Success.

It was smashed in now. He grinned, opened the lid to one of the garbage cans, and swept the debris into the trash container. After he shuffled things around so that the mess wasn't as noticeable, he shut the lid and hung up the sledge. Milo fled the garage, racing back to the house. He forgot to lock the side door and just managed to slip into the kitchen and hang the keys up before his mom found him.

"Oh, here you are," she said. "Are you looking for something to eat, or are you thirsty?"

"I could go for some hot chocolate, Mom."

"Tell you what. Dad and I are going to watch a movie. Why don't you join us? Go ahead and tell Dad to start it. I'll make some cocoa and join you in a bit. I came in to make popcorn, anyway."

"Sure thing, Mom," he said, eager to run off.

He panted, pausing to catch his breath before he got to the family room. When he walked into the room, he called, "Dad, Mom said to start the movie."

"All right," his father said, messing with the DVD remote.

"So what are we gonna see?"

"*The Avengers.*"

"Whoa, super awesome," he shouted.

"I know, right? Too bad your brother isn't here to see this."

Milo smirked. "I get a special treat, and he doesn't. This rules."

His dad smiled.

Matt groaned. He felt like he'd been run over by a semi-truck. What time is it? He rolled over to ask Garrett and discovered that he was gone. Yawning, Matt got up and checked the clock. It was noon. Yikes. He wondered how long Gar had been up. Sauntering downstairs, he heard voices. One was Garrett's. Who's here? Then he recognized Liz's voice. Why's she—he didn't, did he?

"Hi," he greeted, entering the family room.

"Hey, finally up? It's about time," Garrett teased.

"Sorry, Matt. He called me at ten and asked me to come over. When I got here you were still in bed, so we decided to play Mortal Kombat."

"That's fine. You guys eaten? There's still a little bit of Hamburger Helper left."

"I ate before I came," she said.

"You may fix me some, good sir," Garrett answered.

"You know, you could say please," Liz scolded.

"Sorry," he said.

Matt went into the kitchen and Garrett followed.

"So did you tell her?" Matt asked.

"Yep. All of it."

"How'd she take it?"

"Like a chick. She made me promise to let her be by my side during further excursions of danger. I tried to resist her wiles, but she pinned me against the wall and lavished praise upon me until I was weak in the knees," he insisted.

"There's no way that would ever happen. Still. If she wants to be by your side, she must be your true love," Matt mused. "You're lucky."

"I'm aware of this. In her own way, she pointed that out. Though she has a more delicate way than do you, smarty pants."

Matt smirked.

After breakfast, Garrett suggested going to Liz's and finding the camera. "Do you think your parents would mind if we came over?" he added.

"No, but I'd rather not disturb them, because Mom hates being seen when she's as weak as she is. Let's try to hurry in and out."

"All right," Matt said. "You guys wanna help me sweep the house before we go?"

"Mm, but of course, Matthew. It would be our exquisite delight to assist you in this matter," Garrett replied.

It took less than ten minutes for them to clear the house. Matt checked all the doors and windows again to make sure they were locked, especially the deck door. Not that it seems to stop these creeps, he thought. He paused when the phone rang. His heart leapt into his throat as he looked at the caller i.d. It was his mother.

"Guys, I better answer it. It's my mom," he called.

"We'll wait by the front door," Garrett yelled back.

Matt picked up the phone. "Hi, Mom."

"Sweetie, is everything all right? Your dad said you sounded strange when you left your message on his voicemail."

Matt's mouth dried up. He cleared his throat and said, "Oh, it's cool. I was worried when I couldn't get a hold of you. You hadn't called me since you left, so I was concerned."

"What are you talking about? We've called several times, but it seems you're always on the phone. We assumed you're having fun."

"I am, but Mom, I've hardly been on the phone at all."

"Hm, that's weird. Maybe there's a phone off the hook somewhere."

"No. I've called Garrett, Bobby, and Jeff since you've been gone, so there can't be a phone off the hook."

"Maybe it's our phones. We've been having several connection issues with them down here."

"Yeah, maybe," he said, unconvinced that this was the problem.

"Anyway, we're fine. Your dad's gotten you a couple very cool souvenirs, but it's a surprise."

He had the urge to laugh. "Then why did you tell me?"

"Well, you sound so depressed. Getting lonely?"

"A little, but Garrett's been keeping me company, along with Jeff and Bobby."

"As long as you're behaving. Keeping up with your schoolwork?"

"Duh. You know I'm finicky about that."

She chuckled. "Believe me, I know. You get that from me."

He grinned. "Dad wasn't as disciplined with his studies in college, I take it."

"Lord, no. He always wanted to go out. He was a born procrastinator, yet he always buckled down when he had to."

"Sounds like he's changed a lot since then."

"Oh yes. He works so hard. He's really bummed that we couldn't bring you along. It hasn't been the same without you."

Matt felt a tear start at the corner of his eye and quashed it. "I miss you guys, too. But I'm glad you got to go. You deserve a break."

"Thanks for understanding."

"No problem."

"I'm gonna let you go. Your father wants to talk to you. I love you."

"Love you too, Mom."

His father came on the line. "Hey, son. How you doing?"

"Hi, Dad. Doing good. You?"

"Right as rain. But I wish you were here. They had the coolest game shop. You would have been in seventh heaven."

"Aw, cool."

"I got you a game I thought you might like. It's called Enraged."

Matt almost drooled. He'd seen trailers for that online and had watched playthroughs of it on Youtube. It looked super sweet. "Awesome."

"That's not one of the souvenirs, though. You'll find out what those are when we get home."

"Thanks, Dad."

"You're welcome. I gotta go. This phone's about to die. I love you. See ya Thursday."

"See ya. Love you, Dad. Sweet," he yelled as he hung up.

Garrett and Liz came running. "What?" Gar asked.

"My parents are okay. They got me Enraged and some souvenirs."

"Whoa. Your coolness factor just hit its peak."

"So did yours, Gar" Matt retorted.

"Uh, can I ask a question?" Liz said.

"Hon, I believe you just did."

"Shut up, Garrett. Matt, you're always acting like your parents freak you out. What gives?"

He sighed, running a hand through his hair. "I'm a little neurotic. I guess I take after Mom in that respect. My folks are very boisterous, and the loudness grates on my nerves, for some reason. And when they fight, which is a lot, it bothers me. I know it's no big deal. They're passionate about life and work, and they don't agree on a lot, plus running a business together gets tense. I know they love each other, but ever since I can remember, their arguments have always made me super nervous," he admitted.

"I see. But they're not mean or abusive or anything?" Liz asked.

"No. But I do like a warning before they come in the door. They're so loud and chaotic. It's like a whirlwind. It's not their fault, but it just makes me crazy. This is mega embarrassing, and they have no clue."

"Oh. So you guys wanna get going now?" Liz was eager to change the subject. *Poor guy*, she thought, *I had no idea.*

"Let us see if we can find that bloody camera," Garrett agreed.

Matt followed them to Hickory Street, right near the high school. With all the events of the weekend, he was almost delighted to be so close to school. It was comforting, in a way. When they arrived, they managed to get up to Liz's room unnoticed and comb through the small area.

"The camera was clearly high up," Garrett noted as the search began.

He found it taped to the top of the window frame. Garrett placed his thumb over the tiny lens as he ripped the camera from the frame. He glanced at Liz. "See? And you thought I was paranoid when I said you should keep these curtains closed."

"Oh, excuse me. I bow to your unbending wisdom," she retorted.

"Thank you," he said.

"I keep the curtains open in case any other suitors come by," she teased.

"In that case, I'm pretty screwed, aren't I?" he added, winking at her.

"We'd better go now," Matt interrupted, pulling him along.

They got out undetected. Garrett pulled a tack hammer out of his coat pocket.

"Where did that come from?" Matt asked.

"I borrowed it from your dad's tools."

"What? Well, when you're done, give it back. He'd be so miffed if we lost it."

"Psh. He prolly never uses it anyway."

"That's not the point, Gar."

Garrett ignored him as he smacked the tiny camera over and over with the hammer. A low growling noise rose from his mouth. His feverish eyes locked on the camera as he worked. When it was broken at last, Garrett gathered up the pieces and pocketed them.

"I'll get rid of these on my way home," he said.

"How?" Liz asked.

"I'll detour to the train tracks a block over and dispose of them."

"All right. I'll see you at school," she answered, kissing him.

"I love you," he murmured.

"Yeah, yeah, back atcha."

Gar smiled. "Smart mouth."

"Learned it from my muse," she countered.

Matt looked away. "Come on, bro," he interjected.

"Keep your breeches on, Matt."

After yet another goodbye, Garrett was ready to go. He followed Matt to 23 and walked down a block with him, then handed him the tack hammer. "See you tomorrow. You sure you don't need me to walk you home?"

"No. Go see if Milo's doing all right."

Garrett looked at his phone. It was 2:05. "I don't even know if he'll be home. Mom and Dad did say they'd be home late."

"Maybe they got back early."

"Perhaps."

As he left, Matt felt relieved, carefree even. *Maybe I'll watch a movie when I get home,* he decided.

Garrett paused at the railroad tracks. He'd gone a little out of his way to get there, but he was pleased as he scattered the pieces of the camera between the wooden planks. *Here's a nice view for ya, fellas.* A grim smile formed on his face. When this task was done, he continued home. At the front door, he checked the knob and found it unlocked. The moment he entered, he could hear the TV going in the family room. Immediately, he sensed the presence of his family and relaxed. It was on his way into the hall that he wondered why there was a TV in both the family room and basement.

I have one in my room, as do Mom and Dad and even Milo. Hm, are there any other rooms beside the kitchen and bathroom that don't have a television? Oh yeah, the den and the attic. Why do we have some many TVs anyway? He shrugged in response to his random inquiry. *Time to see what that guy was doing on my computer.* He heard Milo laugh as he entered the hall.

Matt shut the TV off and stretched, glancing at the clock. Six o'clock? It seemed much later, perhaps due to the weather. His eyes grew heavy as he leaned back on the couch. He was watching for the clock to change to 6:01, when he dropped off into sleep and found himself at some sort of grade school bizarre, surrounded by tables and booths selling various items. Wandering through the cafeteria, where the booths and tables began, he felt compelled forward into the gym, where more booths awaited. At last, he stopped at one and looked around. A very old Native American woman stood behind him.

As he gazed at the animal books on her shelves, she began chanting. One of the books commanded his attention. It had a black wolf with pale yellow eyes on the cover. He flipped through the book, hypnotized by the woman's chanting. He couldn't understand what she was saying, for she was speaking in her native language, but it seemed important. He stopped thumbing through the book and put it back, turning toward her. For a slit second, he suspected her of trying to mesmerize him into buying something. Instead, she tapped his shoulder.

"Protect, dog, protect," she ordered in a murmur. Her eyes bore into him, piercing him with hidden meaning.

Matt gasped. At that moment, he knew what he had to do. The knowledge he'd gained was indescribable, because he couldn't put it into words or even think it out. But something deep within knew of a plan of which he was consciously unaware. He left the booth. Somehow, he was a wolf now: black with pale yellow eyes gleaming. He raced through a forest. Above him, a bald eagle screeched, leading the way. He panted. The eagle glided down in front of him as they came to a clearing.

Here, a woman lay on the ground. A man stood above her, beating on her. Snarling, Matt attacked the man, knocking him down and biting his arms. He could see that he must have fought this man before, because the man had bite marks on his ankles and shins.

The fiend shrieked at the woman, "He can't protect you forever. He can't always be with you."

A split second later, the dream changed. Now he was kneeling in front of a double-edged sword. He paid little attention to his surroundings, except to note that he seemed to be kneeling on a broken, rocky ground, engulfed in a royal purple fog. He gazed at the sword, its brass hilt gleaming. The fog brightened. It came to him that this sword was two different things in one. First, it was the truth. Second, it was his destiny. He was at a crossroads, and he didn't know whether he would pick up the sword or not. Fraught with indecision, all he could do was stare, awestruck and frozen.

Though he seemed to be alone, he heard a voice whisper through the fog. The voice was quiet and rife with authority but somehow comforting.

"To defeat the king in the shadows and reclaim my throne, you must accept your mission. You will be required to sacrifice. Trade your gift for your enemy. A blanket of snow you must spread over him as one would a homemade quilt of endless value."

"How do I find the king?" he asked, though he had no idea what any of this meant.

"One will lead to the other," was the response.

As he listened, the scent of spring filled his nostrils. He could taste cool, refreshing rain in his mouth. Warm, soothing serenity flooded him. His eyes fluttered open and closed as he was swept up in another dream.

Garrett didn't get it. He'd checked everything on his computer and could see nothing unusual. The history had been cleared on his browser, so he had no idea what the man might have been looking up, if anything. *I guess there's nothing to be done about it, then.* He paused, hand on his chin. *Maybe I should search for hidden cameras.* Half an hour later, he was satisfied that his room was clear and joined the others in the family room.

"Hi, honey," his mom greeted.

"When did you get back?" his father inquired.

"A little bit ago. You guys are home early."

"Yeah. It didn't take as long as we expected," his mother explained.

"What didn't?"

"Nothing that concerns you," his father added. A stern look came into his eyes.

"Oh, okay," Garrett said.

"Hey, Gar, wanna sit by me?" Milo asked.

"Sure." He ruffled Milo's hair.

"Knock it off," he protested. "We're watching *The Avengers*."

"I can see that. Hey, how come you have cocoa?"

Milo stuck his tongue out.

"Go make yourself some if you want," their mother told him.

"Maybe I will."

Garrett headed for the kitchen. As he opened the cabinet to grab a cup, he happened to glance out the back door. The side door to the garage was ajar. Okay, no, he thought, almost knocking the bottom row of glasses and cups off the shelf. He grabbed one and set it on the counter. Then he went out to shut the garage door. Before he closed it, however, he went in to poke around. He checked to see if his father's car was there. It was. Everything seemed normal, so he stepped out, missing the fact that the hand sledge hung askew on the pegboard. Garrett reached in, locked the door, and slammed it shut. Shaking his head, he went back to the kitchen.

He was about to mix the cocoa, when it dawned on him that perhaps he should search Milo's room for cameras as well. Darn it. *I've got to search this whole bloody house now.*

Matt awoke at eight. Yawning, he got up and checked all the doors and windows downstairs, confirming that they were locked. Next, he hurried down to the basement. He was unafraid as he went through each room. *No one here,* he thought, yawning again. At last, he meandered upstairs and checked every room, door, window, and closet. *Good, the upstairs is clear, and the deck door is still bolted*

tight. A creak issued from the attic above. He was used to the attic floor settling like that, but he went up there anyway. Two minutes later, he was back in his room. The house was locked up tight, and no one was lying in wait. Somehow, this doesn't surprise me, he realized.

Given his prior experience, perhaps he should have been wary. Tonight, though, he hummed as he got ready for bed, more certain than ever of his safety. Tomorrow, he would be glad to return to school. I'm even looking forward to seeing Brandenburg, he mused. Wow, that is sad. He shook his head. After he brushed his teeth, he put his IPOD in the docking station and pressed play. Soon, he was meandering in and out of a light doze. At one point, he thought a shadow hovered over him, but he was suddenly so groggy, he couldn't be sure. In no time, he was out.

Buster tried to follow his earthly master out the door. He howled and whined until his master clamped a hand over his muzzle.

"No, Buster. I've got to go out, and you cannot come. You be good and guard the house," Lawrence Welker demanded.

Buster sat by the door, his head drooping.

"You are the most sensitive dog I've ever worked with. Now honestly, I'm not trying to hurt your feelings, but I've got work to do. Stay," he said as he walked out the door.

Buster obeyed, eyeing him with a wounded expression as he closed the door. Lawrence glided off the porch. He had his night attire on. Time to get down to business, he thought as he climbed up the ladder toward the Marshalls' deck door. He smiled. You really have to admire the kid's guts. It's a shame I've got to keep him from investigating further into these matters. Almost seems unfair.

To be continued…

Epilogue

Sixty Years Prior (1952)

SEVENTEEN-YEAR-OLD MARAH SORI saw his childhood slipping away. His innocence was almost gone. He resented his friends, for he was no longer like them. He didn't care about friendship and childish longings. They believed you could hold on to these things. But there was no such thing as innocence. The fools, he thought. Love and joy and hate, such simple concepts, were out of his grasp now. The world was a lie, and he was determined to expose it.

Little did he realize that hatred was what he felt, and it was hollowing him out, rotting him until only a lust for power remained. He did not long for power so that he might protect others or so that he would no longer be helpless. Far from it. He chased after it so he could destroy others and the world of foolishness in which they participated. He would show them the truth, all right. There was no sense of responsibility to hinder him. Destruction was his goal. It was the only thing. He would become a monster in their eyes and, in doing so, would expose their falsehoods.

He couldn't wait to look in their eyes, theirs full of supplicant tears, his full of rage. He would tear pleas from their lips and sneer, and in his malice, he would call back to them, "Don't you recognize the one you've made? Do you see what you created? How do you like the new me, the consequence of all your love, your compassion, your stupidity?"

He roiled to think that each one would envision a day when he would see things their way. A day when he would return and proclaim that they were right, that love was the only thing that mattered. Wretched peasants, your pseudo-innocence and ill-equipped joy shall be your ruination, he mused. These venomous ideas formulated, he returned to his dark work. He was a full sixty years away from knowing that an obstacle to his domination would arise in the form of a fifteen-year-old boy named Matthew Christopher Marshall.

www.ingramcontent.com/pod-product-compliance
Lightning Source LLC
LaVergne TN
LVHW021047100526
838202LV00079B/4664